The Child
Who Never
Was

A Bronnie Browne Mystery

Erin Roberts

The Child Who Never Was

This novel was printed using the Dylexie font to improve accessibility.

Printed in the United States of America
First Edition, 2018
Print ISBN 978-0692-18743-2
EPUB ISBN 978-0692-18744-9

To my beloved, John, for all of the endless encouragement. And for bankrolling this.

Prologue:
November 2009

He appeared to be your average businessman, except that he was dozing face down in a half-eaten turkey sandwich. The way that the leaf of lettuce would float up to the sleeper's mouth when he inhaled and then flutter away when he exhaled was almost comical, while sounds from his snoring reverberated off the walls of the tiny bungalow.

The bastard was still wearing his dark business suit complete with what had been a meticulously pressed shirt and tie, but they were now crumpled and speckled with mustard.

We paused at the doorway to the kitchen, observing him in silence. I wanted to laugh at how ridiculous he looked but did not dare to.

Barefoot and cautious, holding my small five year old to my chest, I tiptoed through the living room, "Heel to toe, quietly..." repeating the phrase in my mind. My baby didn't stir and even in her current slumber she never let go of her stuffed bear. It's dark purple velvet now faded and worn in patches. The only movement made, besides the steady rising and lowering of her chest was the bobbing of the dark curls on her head.

I hesitated at the front door. The barrier between our old life and the new.

The metal storm door had always been noisy, creaking and groaning with every pull, clanging like an ill-tuned bell when closed. It was really the only option, though. All of the windows had been nailed shut long ago and the rear door could only be opened with a key. The front it had to be.

Almost half a can of lubricant had been sacrificed on the hinges alone and, thankfully, it opened with little protest. Only a muffled "beep beep" from the security system panel, which had been relegated to a drawer to deaden the sound, made any protest to our exit.

Sliding my feet into ballet flats on the doorstep, I tugged a scarf from my shoulders to cover my dark hair. A patchy, primer gray, unmarked van sat idling three doors down. Its headlights flashed once. I went gingerly down the steps, and around to the side of the house. I knelt as best I could under the load of my daughter and retrieved a small duffle bag from behind a bush and slung it over the shoulder that was not cradling my sleeping girl.

Careful to stay in the grass away from the few street lights, we darted towards the waiting van.

A giant more than a man, at least six and a half feet tall and appearing almost as wide, with brown skin and tribal tattoos on his neck got out of the passenger's seat and slid open the side door. Relieved and grateful, I think something that might have almost been a smile fluttered briefly across my face.

He took the duffel bag from my shoulder and helped me lay my daughter on the long bench seat in the van with practiced ease.

I placed my hand on her head when she began to stir. "It's ok, back to sleep little one."

The giant tossed the bag on the floor behind our bench, closed the sliding door, and took one last inspection of the quiet block. He got back in and motioned to the driver, who was so similar in appearance they might have been brothers. They wasted no time turning around in the middle of the deserted road and left the perfect neighborhood behind.

None of us looked back.

Chapter 1

Giving myself a quick last-minute look in the mirror had revealed not only white schmutz on the shoulder of my brother's old sweatshirt directly above the Pacific Beach surf logo, but also a muddy paw print from our poodle on my shorts, a freshly opened scab on my shin and my long bangs suddenly deciding the 1970s flip was back in fashion.

Hoping that my appearance suggested more of a misfit bohemian vibe than a vagrant hobo, I made my way out the door. A better first impression might benefit me since it was my first day of a new school, but being a guy I'm generally allowed a certain amount of fashion latitude.

The lumbering yellow bus was only sparsely filled with kids by the time it wheezed on my street. I leaned on the old real estate sign still littering our front yard and toyed with a soccer ball, trying to look casual as my ride came to a stop at the curb. By contrast, my stomach was a nervous wreck and totally full of butterflies.

Not literally full of butterflies, of course. That would be disconcerting.

Up until this point, I had only rarely ridden a school bus. A student who had never been subject to the infamous cheese wagon was sure to make me an anomaly in this part of the world. Thankfully there was an empty seat behind a curly haired girl and I wiggled my way down the aisle to it, dodging a gum wrapper used as a projectile and stepping over someone's outstretched leg as I went. Most kids try to get to the back seats, but the less time I had to walk the gauntlet, the better.

Sinking into the green bench, I smelled its ancient vinyl upholstery, mixed with the scents of pine air freshener, exhaust fumes, and sweaty kids. I instantly missed the other towns where they didn't have school buses, or my parents wouldn't allow me to ride them. I got glared at, hit with a paper airplane and nauseous all before we made it three blocks. Yep, riding the bus was entirely overrated.

We labored our way through tree-lined streets of the town on the way to school. Adorable cottages and three-story Colonial columned estates competed for attention. No matter their size, they almost all boasted porches, manicured lawns and parents pushing jogging strollers.

Idyllic for parents. Boring for kids.

While we discuss boredom, I can tell you our school was no different in its lack of character. Captain's Watch School was your typical brick 1950s era schoolhouse. Arranged in a reverse Z shape, it was a one level, lackluster building that remarkably looked almost exactly like the other two schools I had attended in my short career as a student. In fact, it probably looked like 90 percent of all of the schools in the country, down to the ubiquitous surrounding soccer fields and playgrounds. It was as though school systems all bought the same building plans from the same depressing school-building megastore.

The store probably sold stinky school buses too.

Two things made this school different from the others I attended. One was the view. The building commanded the top of the hill in town, allowing one to see over the treetops, past our neighborhood towards the harbor. Long docks and boats stretched along the waterfront. The masts of sailboats bobbed up and down on the gray water, making a perfect perch for seagulls.

It was a sight that reminded me of the town where I was born and spent the first six years of my life. They were vague memories, but comforting nonetheless. Even if we were on the opposite coast with no surfing to be had for miles.

But I digress, like anyone our age gives a rat's ass about the lovely view from detention.

The second difference worthy of note was that this was the first combined school I had attended. Diminutive kindergarteners filled the front of the bus while bearded middle schoolers strode to the rear. We were spared attending with the high school kids as they were shipped off to the consolidated monstrosity at the center of the county.

The bus had been oddly half empty for the ride in and now pulling to parking circle I could see why. The lots were positively overflowing with parents personally driving their beloved children to their doom. They were backed out onto the residential streets, even to the public park across the road. The sight made me uneasy; our ride home would be much more crowded for sure. Getting a seat this afternoon would probably require equal parts diplomacy, deception, and speed.

Last week's orientation was a chance to meet the teachers, see your home classroom and, if you have those parents who are on top of their game, drop off your already purchased school supplies. My parents are never on top of their game, so this morning I was hauling my backpack full of last-minute supplies purchased in a mad dash to the only office supply store three towns over.

At least I knew how to get to class. I went straight down the long hallway in the middle of the "Z," past the library and to the first classroom on the left. "Andrews" was written in cursive in the middle of the otherwise unremarkable door.

Mrs. Andrews was just inside, shaking hands as we entered. Her smile framed by cherry red lips was friendly, but she was a physically intimidating specimen, with a build so massive that she almost filled the doorframe. Her red rockabilly hairstyle barely made it through the opening.

Mental note of the day: Don't make the teacher angry or she will squash me like the little bug that I am.

Mrs. Andrews strode to the front of the room as the bell rang. "Now my minions, first-day paperwork for you." She gestured to a stack of multicolored sheets of paper in her left hand. "And your first class assignment." She presented a top hat in her right hand.

Weaving through the rows of desks, she stopped by each to greet the students, give them papers and have them pick something from within the top hat. The seats were arranged in five rows of four. This was the fewest number of students I'd had in a class I since Kindergarten. Maybe even preschool.

Our teacher continued speaking as she walked. "I know most of you are returning students from last year and in this small town, you've probably known most of your classmates your whole life. That said, there is always a chance to meet someone new, or learn something different." She grinned as she got to the girl with curly hair, the one who had been in front of me on the bus and now was seated in the desk to my right.

As Mrs. Andrews finished her rounds, kids began to peer about the room, looking for the faces belonging to the names on the paper slips they had pulled from the top hat. My paper read "Bronwyn Browne."

It wouldn't do me any good to gaze around. Everyone in the class was a stranger to me. So I figured that I'd wait until the bell rang and maybe the last person standing would be my interview partner.

I felt a tap on my shoulder. It was the girl on my right. She gestured to my paper. "That is me."

Her bright green eyes struck me first. A purple headband held her dark brown ringlets back so that her eyes stood out against her chestnut colored skin. Some of her long curls reached her shoulders, stretching looser as they got longer.

We agreed to interview one another at lunch, so I followed her later to the cafeteria. Her white dress shirt, which was buttoned all the way to the neck, cuff links, small pearl earrings, and a silver charm bracelet, stood out against the graphic t-shirts and sweats of our classmates.

"Hi," I said as we sat down across from each other, both of us carrying lunch boxes and skipping the long line for buying what was sure to be questionable school food.

"Good morning, Sean."

My anxiety climbed. She was gazing at me in a way that I felt as though my face was imprinting on her brain, studying me.

We sat there in silence.

Finally, she relaxed her shoulders and gaze, opened her lunch and inquired "Are you all settled in?"

"Settled into what?"

"Your new house, new school. Are you feeling settled?"

"Totally."

Her face was quizzical. "Really?"

"No, not really." I confided.

"Me neither."

Something occurred to me. "How did you know my name is Sean?"

She glanced at her fingernails. "It is written on your desk, your backpack and," pointed to the table in front of me, "on your lunch box."

I looked down to notice that my dad had, in fact, written my name in black permanent marker in very large, almost illegible script. No doubt he was hoping that I might not lose my lunch box again this year. Fat chance.

"Ah." I responded, feeling a tad idiotic. Not helping my case further, I blurted out. "You have an accent."

"Everyone has an accent." She said coolly.

"I mean, you have a non-American accent. Where are you from?"

"I've lived in quite a few countries, though my parents are from England, West London to be exact." She took a bite of a small, crustless sandwich and watched me intently as I opened a container holding my bean burrito.

I waited for Bronwyn to interview me, but she didn't. "What brought you to America?" I tried to imitate her gaze, probably unsuccessfully because she wrinkled her forehead and narrowed her eyes at me.

"My father's company transferred him here."

I started to ask what he did for a living, but she set down her sandwich and held up her hand signaling me not to talk.

"Interviewing people is often uncomfortable. To save time, may I answer all of your questions you have on that paper and we can get back to eating?"

Bronwyn launched into a monologue.

"My father is a computer engineer. My mother specializes in large-scale fundraising and event planning, usually for charities or schools. I have one older brother, Michael. He stayed at his boarding school in England. I don't participate in any team sports, but study fencing and various martial arts. Violin is my instrument of choice, classical guitar a close second. The Godfather Part II, Steinbeck, sushi, and decaf caramel macchiato."

She took a large bite of her sandwich, leaving me in shock scrambling to write it all down. Remarkably, Bronnie answered every question that I had written on my paper, in order, except the last one.

After a big gulp from her water bottle and the belch that followed, she continued. "And I had a pet dog, but he had to stay in England."

A fleeting thought that perhaps Bronnie was psychic was followed by me writing *Left pet dog and brother in England* as the last notes on my interview sheet.

Probably I should phrase that differently.

We sat in silence for a few minutes, me eating my burrito, her taking notes in a small black leather bound journal. This moment must be what awkward blind dates are like for adults.

Second mental note of the day: Never go on a blind date. Especially with psychics.

I opened my mouth to ask another question, she answered me first.

"People call me Bronnie."

Definitely psychic.

"Aren't you going to ask me any questions?"

"No need, I already know enough about you to complete this class exercise."

Yep, maybe I'd write off dating altogether, blind and otherwise. I looked up and down our lunch table at the rest of our classmates, who were all busy with their interviews.

Everyone was busy with work except two boys, who had caught the gaze of the cafeteria police for tossing grapes into each other's mouths.

"Are you sure you don't have any questions? I think we have to present this."

"I'm sure," Bronnie replied with finality in her voice.

Later, back in class, I presented my information about Bronnie. Then I got the opportunity to wonder with fear and fascination, how she would describe me, considering that she had asked me no questions.

Bronnie went to the front of the class, stood straight in her dark jeans and white dress shirt. She gestured to me with an open hand and started speaking.

"Class, I would like to introduce you to Sean Watkins. He is new to this school, recently moving from the south and before that, California. His father is a doctor with the new office on Water Street. He has an older brother in high school and a baby sibling at home. They also have a pet dog, a standard poodle."

Bronnie turned to me, and we locked eyes for a moment as if she were searching in my mind for something. "He plays soccer and is learning to skateboard."

My jaw must have been on the floor as Bronnie made her way back to her desk. I watched in awe as she sat down and leaned back casually in her chair. She gave me sideways glance but then her eyes glazed over, and she slowly turned her attention to the front of the room.

When the bell rang at the end of the day, we bus riders filed out of the classroom first, ahead of the car riders.

Bronnie was fast, seated well before me, so I went right up to her bench.

"Can I sit here?" I asked.

"You may." She replied.

Ignoring the dig at my grammar, I sat down. "How did you do it? Are you a mind reader?"

"Hah!" She chuckled. "Hardly. I am merely observant."

"So tell me how you did it. What did you see to make you realize all of those things about me without asking a single question."

She took two lollipops from her book bag and offered me one, then removed the paper from her own.

"Thanks," I said, accepting it. "Like, how did you know that I'm new here?"

"Well, I saw you walk to the bus stop this morning. There were two cars in your driveway with West Virginia license plates. This state requires a person to register their car and get new plates within 30 days of moving, so I concluded you've just moved. Your family could be military, allowing you to keep your car registered in another state, but as there are not many military bases in West Virginia, that hypothesis would be unlikely. Also, a wooden sign holder, the kind that estate agents use, is still in your garden."

"Pretty good, but how did you know I was originally from California?"

"Your accent, or lack of an accent. You have West Virginia license plates, but no mountain drawl. Your hair is also longer than ninety percent of the boys here. That is not something usual in this area. The dead giveaway, though, was that I heard you use the word 'totally' your everyday speech. You were serious, so concluded that you had lived out west, most likely the southern part." She licked her lollipop. "Plus your sweatshirt from a San Diego surf company added to the equation, most likely having been a hand me down since it is too big for you yet well worn."

She paused for a moment. "But more intriguing was your lunch."

"My burrito?" I asked.

Bronnie nodded. "Not may east coast kids can stand the look of refried beans. I realized that when our family went out for tacos last week."

"Suppose so...How did you know my brother was in high school?"

Bronnie smiled, "That was easy, no one got on the bus with you this morning, plus the old sweatshirt. Having an older brother already and a baby in the house would be quite an unusual age gap."

"My mom would definitely agree. How did you know about my sister and our dog?" I asked.

"You have white spit up on your shoulder." She pointed out the schmutz on my sweatshirt from where I had burped Margot that morning before leaving to catch the bus. Then she moved her hand to point at my leg.

"There is a muddy paw print on your shorts, but no dog hair on your clothes. It is unlikely someone would be fastidious enough to remove dog hair from their clothes, but not mud. So it is highly likely that your dog doesn't shed. Few dogs with a paw size that large are non-shedders. The most common household pet of that type is a standard poodle. I guessed."

"A good guess," I said.

"As for the hobbies, someone left a skateboard on the porch. Plus you have multiple small bruises and scrapes on your shins, a typical injury from practicing kickflips." She started to get her bag ready; her stop was coming up. "Hmm. The bus driver appears to be doing our stops in the reverse order from the morning."

"Soccer?" I asked.

"You left your ball out front." She winked at me. "You should try to clean up after yourself. Your home looks like, what do they call it over here? When families sell unwanted items at their home?"

"A yard sale?"

"Yes. A yard sale."

"I'll have to remember that. See you tomorrow?"

She raised her eyebrows, swaying gently backward as the bus came to a halt.

"Tomorrow you can tell me what I had for dinner, or what movie I watched."

"Love to. Though I'm guessing you will be eating tacos tonight since it is Tuesday."

Bronnie left the bus quickly and scooted across the street to a historic yellow colonial on the corner. She was through the gate of the picket fence before the bus turned for my street.

Chapter 2

I was in the middle of making salsa for (you guessed it) taco Tuesday when my dad came home from the clinic.

"Hey my man." He dropped a briefcase on the desk and gave me a hug around the shoulders with one arm and grabbed a beer from the fridge with the other. "Salsa smells good, as usual."

"Thanks. Mom said we are having fish tacos, so I'm throwing some mango and pineapple in this time."

"Perfect." He hummed. "She still working?"

Right about now Margot decided she was no longer happy in her bouncer with dad home and let us know with a cry that sounded like an air raid siren. Dad ignored the noise and picked her up. They both sat at the table kitchen table why she giggled happily on his knee, trying desperately to chew on the cold bottle in dad's hand.

"Still too young for that, Mar." I said to her as if she understood me.

She cooed at me and chewed some more on the glass.

My mom appeared out of nowhere behind my dad and kissed him on top of the head. She was silent, like a ninja, but we were used to it. "Hello, Dr. Watkins." She said and then tousled Margot's baby hair.

"Hello to you, Dr. Watkins." Dad replied.

That was a new favorite interaction between my parents as my dad's becoming a doctor had been something of a midlife crisis career change and he had only recently completed medical school. Mom's doctorate was in something else entirely, not medicine, but it was a fun compliment they paid to one another.

Moving to the fridge, mom took ingredients out for dinner. "Thanks for making salsa again, Sean." She kissed me on the cheek and I put the last of the mango in the container with the other ingredients. "I still don't know why onions don't make you cry like everyone else."

"Contacts." I said, gesturing to my eyes.

She nodded, "Well we can be thankful something good is coming of your terrible vision. Want to help with the fish?"

Margot, as if on cue, had tired of dad and was now reaching for me. Spoiled, that one. "Nah, I'll play with the baby. Dad can be sous chef."

Digging a bag of chips out of the pantry, he made sure to try the salsa a few times before breading the fish. "So how was the first day of school?"

"Decent. It is weird having such a small school and tiny classes. I think I made a friend, though, a girl up the street. She is new too." Margot did not coo at this news, jealousy must start early.

"Oh?" Mom said, "Where she is from?"

"England, kind of. She said they have moved a lot, like us. But she sounds English."

My dad chimed in. "Another family of nomads. What's she like?"

"Um," I stalled, not knowing how to describe Bronnie without making her sound like a psycho. "She's really smart, kind of quiet, plays the violin and likes the Godfather. We had to interview each other. She has super curly hair and really green eyes."

My mom gave my dad a sly look which I knew was code for "I wonder if Sean has a girlfriend."

"Ugh, not like that, mom."

"I didn't say a word." She mumbled and tossed a fish filet into a hot skillet, making it sizzle. "Does anyone know if Sebastian will be gracing us with his presence?"

My dad tried to talk with a mouth full of chips. "Lacrosse until eight. Save him a plate."

The next day, Bronnie was there on the bus sitting at the window. I took the liberty of parking myself next to her.

She just nodded and turned to look out the window some more. After a few minutes, she spoke to me. "You never asked me how I knew your father was a doctor."

"Oh, that one at least I already knew. I like to help my dad at his office. Your file was on his desk the day when you came in for your school physical." Score one for Sean.

"Is it your goal to be a doctor one day?"

"Maybe." I shrugged, "A surgeon if anything. Don't think I'd have the patience for general practice."

"I suppose I don't know much about the day to day life of either profession." She mused.

"Ow," I blurted as something sharp tagged me in the back of the skull. It happened a second time and I heard a giggle from the kid in the seat behind ours. I didn't know him, but he was bigger than me, and probably stupider. Ah, the joys of a full school bus.

Finally, after a third jab, Bronnie turned and glared at the guy. She didn't say a word. There must have been some venom in those green eyes. The boy took a deep breath, but immediately sat back in his seat, and finally left me in peace.

As we got closer to school, though, his boredom must have returned because so did the poking. When the bus finally did pull up to the school, I stood up immediately. Much as I would have liked to put space between myself and Pokey-finger, I stepped back slightly to allow Bronnie into the aisle ahead of me.

Ladies first.

Taking time to be the gentleman meant that Pokey-finger bumped into me, probably as a matter of principal. I didn't get a good look at him but could tell he was not very tall, but somehow he felt more imposing. He stayed uncomfortably close as we exited allowing me to get a whiff of various body odors.

Bully morning breath, fabulous. Bronnie stole a quick glance at my tormenter over my shoulder, and we filed out of the bus.

This genius with the overactive finger now had a small posse of lesser bullies to watch him annoy me as we made our way to class. I'd encountered obnoxious kids before in my other schools, but you'd be surprised at how much they could vary from location to location.

I mean a bully in a largely Buddhist community in San Diego is very different from one in deep Appalachia. Taking a page from my mom's job in international studies, I always tried to observe the techniques and personalities of offensive kids before responding. Some kids had no desire to get into an actual physical fight and merely wanted to intimidate. Others had no problem whatsoever with going straight into a brawl.

This is what I was contemplating when all traffic in the hall stopped short to allow a line of well-behaved lilliputian students through the crowd on their way to the lower school wing.

It was then that I heard a loud cry behind me and turned to see Pokeyfinger on one knee with his right hand bent up and back towards his shoulder. Bronnie's delicate brown fingers were wrapped around his, pulling his hand up by his ear at an angle that was apparently rather painful. It would appear that Bronnie did not give a crap about the nuances of local bully culture.

She very calmly whispered in his ear, "I do not appreciate you antagonizing my friend."

No sooner had she finished speaking this sentence then Mrs. Andrews, hearing and seeing some commotion, threaded through the crowd toward us. Her dark hair was done up in a 1950's style pompadour complete with era-appropriate handkerchief; her do bobbing and swaying as she walked.

"Is everything ok over here?" She asked, standing in a superhero power pose with her legs apart and hands on her hips.

Bronnie deftly switched her grip so that she held Pokey-finger's hand in her own and pulled him up to his feet.

"Oh, I think he just stumbled when traffic stopped moving. I was helping him up." Bronnie was all green eyes and innocence towards the teacher then turned around released the bully's hand from her own. Her eyes were cold and calculating now, but her voice was smooth. "Are you quite alright?"

He grunted, brushed off his jeans, and then stumbled down the hall.

"He is probably more embarrassed than anything. It being the second day of school and all." I said, trying to smooth things over.

Mrs. Andrews put her arm on Bronnie's, "The bigger they are the harder they fall. Now, my minions, you two get a move on."

"You are one of a kind, Bronnie," I said to her when we were out of earshot of our teacher.

"Thanks, Sean. If you'd like, I can teach you some of my moves so he doesn't bother you again."

"Oh, I've got some moves." Throwing some fake karate chops. "I'm just not as eager to use them."

"Pacifist?"

"Something like that."

Later that day, when walking to art class, we passed a line of our first projects themed "Mixed Media Summer Vacation". Collages comprised of magazine pictures, postcards and other bits of media were tacked carefully to a strip of cork board along the hallway.

As we neared the end of the row, Bronnie slowed, almost at a stop. Turning her head and searching way we had just come, then towards the front again with eyes narrowed. I very nearly ran into the back of her.

Attempting to follow her gaze, "What's up?" I whispered.

"Hm. Nothing." She shook her head and continued with the rest of the class, but taking one last glance at the projects before turning the corner.

Interlude:
April 19, 2010

"Ok, one last story, munchkin." I stroked my daughter's dark, silky curls, her little head tucked tight against my shoulder. Halfway through the repetition of the same words we read every night, she dozed and I slid carefully out from under her weight.

Closing the door to our dormitory, I slipped on my shower shoes and padded quietly down the hall to the communal bathroom carrying a basket full of toiletries in hand. Just like college would have been, or maybe the military, if I had followed either of those paths instead of the one I took. A dark skinned teenager with a small diamond nose stud held the bathroom door open for me.

Two other families on their floor had just found homes, so the bathroom was empty at this time of night. The shower steamy and welcoming. Shampoo stung my knuckles, which were raw and red from weeks of training.

I barely recognized myself these days. Bags under my eyes, spit ends and perpetually bitten nails, but none of that mattered. My daughter was safe, if only temporarily, that was the only goal. The past six months had been brutal, but in a better way than the past six years.

A familiar buzz briefly filled the speakers, announcing the 9:00 night lockdown. Now the only people who could get past the two security doors and night guard were residents who worked late.

Standing at the mirror I surveyed my dark hair, knowing that tomorrow it would be different. Everything would be different. That is, if the courts allowed it. Would the bastard even show up for the proceedings. No one had seen him in months, no summons had reached him, and no arrests had been made.

Even so, the nerves were too much for me to stand and I took a swig from a bottle that looked like perfume. All kinds of alcohol and drugs were forbidden in the dorm, but sometimes the mothers found a way around the rule. Like putting a little rum into an empty perfume bottle, which made the rum taste vaguely like gardenia.

"Tomorrow." I whispered to the figure in the mirror. "Tomorrow we start over."

Chapter 3

There are days when you begin to realize that maybe you should have just stayed in bed. One Monday had that feeling when Bronnie and I descended our bus stairs as usual, but into a very different atmosphere than we were used to.

Huddled at the entrance to our school were the head custodian, a few teachers (including our Mrs. Andrews), the principal, the office secretary and a police officer. They were agitated. Our principal stood at the center like a quarterback, her arms crossed while she inspected arriving students and listened to the hushed whispers of the surrounding adults. Occasionally she nodded.

We locked eyes for a brief second and, even though I hadn't done anything officevisit-worthy, she gave chills down my spine just the same.

Bronnie watched them intently as we made our way through the doors. Her curls bobbed along merrily, contrasting against her bright turquoise pea coat.

"I wonder what is going on?" I mused, turning for one last glance at the entry.

"Some excitement for once, I hope."

Bronnie was even happily humming by the time we got to class, but it so starkly contrasted with the nervous calm of the other students she quickly stopped. She took out a lollipop instead, being apparently the only person in the school invigorated by the arrival of police officers.

Finally, after what seemed like an hour, but was probably closer to ten minutes, Mrs. Andrews strode into the room. As morning announcements began, we were startled to see our principal on the projection screen instead of the usual kids from the A/V club.

Mrs. Duncan was standing before the camera in an over-starched black and white pantsuit. Her hair was a silvery, flawlessly styled updo. A massive stone necklace, an electronic watch, and manicured nails completed the look of someone who might have been running a billion-dollar corporation rather than a small town school.

Her speech had all of the warmth of a post-apocalyptic dictator. "Good morning students. No doubt today you have noticed something is amiss at our school. This weekend, an unknown perpetrator took it upon him or herself to vandalize one of our classrooms. I am sure most of you feel as distressed as your administrators."

"Hardly." Someone behind me mumbled. I gave a cursory look around to emphasize to Mrs. Andrews that it had not been me.

The principal, unfortunately, continued. "Our school is like a second home for us and, as such, should always be treated with respect and dignity."

From any other person that might have sounded plausible. Blah blah.

She took a deep breath. "We have video evidence of the culprit, breaking into one of our cottages." (Cottages were the term the school used for the ugly trailers separate from the building that served for extra classrooms. As though calling them something cute made them cute. It didn't work. They were still ugly.) "...and we are giving the perpetrator an opportunity to come forward of their own volition. If the guilty party chooses to turn themselves in, the punishment may be less severe."

"*May* be. Notice she didn't say 'will be'." Bronnie observed.

I glanced at my friend while there was another pause on the monitor. The dead air was probably for emphasis, but principal spoke as though she were on a video chat instead of a one-way broadcast. You could have heard crickets playing chess in our room it was so quiet.

Bronnie scanned our teacher, who was glaring at little Jamie Caldwell, who in turn was glaring at the floor.

The silence had been so complete that I jumped when the person on the screen spoke again, "And if there are any other students with information about this crime, I would urge you to please speak up as well. That is all."

The camera swung abruptly to some very anxious students from the A/V club who did their best to continue usual morning announcements. I don't think anyone in our class listened; we were all looking at Mrs. Andrews or Jamie.

Our teacher finally spoke when the screen went gray. "Jamie Caldwell." She boomed, startling the class, causing pencils and various other objects to hit the ground.

A muffed curse came from Matt de la Rosa's corner of the room as he proceeded to retrieve the contents of his entire pencil box from the floor.

Meanwhile, Jamie peered up at the teacher like a deer caught in headlights. "Yes, ma'am?" he managed to choke out.

Now that she looked him in the eyes, her former countenance of anger changed to something like confusion mixed with pity. "Do you have anything you want to tell me?"

Jamie took searched the room for support or perhaps an exit plan. His eyes met Bronnie's while he answered the teacher, "No, ma'am."

Mrs. Andrews heels clicked on the way to her desk where she retrieved a hall pass and held it out to him. "Fine. You can try your luck with Mrs. Duncan."

Poor Jamie's mouth fell open and emitted a sound as though he'd just been punched in the gut. After a beat he straightened himself, rose from the desk and, like a criminal destined for the gallows, took the pass from our teacher.

Bronnie's hand immediately shot up into the air.

Our teacher reluctantly tilted her head in our direction. "Yes, Miss Browne."

Uh oh, I thought, *she is using last names.*

"Sean and I would like to go with Jamie to the principal's office." She blurted.

"We what?" I was stunned.

Mrs. Andrews was astonished. "Why on earth would you want to do that?"

"Because Sean and I were part of it." Bronnie confessed.

"We what?" I repeated, in complete disbelief.

Jamie had a look of bewilderment on his face that must have rivaled my own. Our teacher was clearly not convinced. The two model students seemed about as likely to mastermind school vandalism as our class pet hamster, Carrot McFuzziface.

Not in the mood to argue however, Mrs. Andrews let her momentary fatigue get the better of her. "Fine, the three of you can go to the principal's office together and sort this out."

Bronnie leapt out of her desk and was at the door before I could even finish my exasperated sigh. Before Jamie could ask what the heck was going on. Before Mrs. Andrews could write a hall pass.

She practically sprinted to the principal's office leaving Jamie and me content to stroll in her wake. Glancing down in his direction, because he was a good three inches shorter, I realized how pitiful he looked. Tripping on his hems of his old corduroy pants, he questioned, no one in particular, why on earth Bronnie volunteered to go to the office and again, why she was so damned happy about it.

"Because she is insane." I ventured.

We trudged. She power walked.

We rounded the corner at the end of the hall and practically ran into Bronnie who had come to an abrupt halt at a now of our most recent art projects. Again.

Out of nowhere, she asked, "How many kids are in our grade?"

I rubbed the back of my neck like my dad does when my mom is driving him crazy. "I don't know, about forty."

She didn't turn her attention from the wall. "There are 18 kids in our class. County regulations stipulate no more than 24 per class. I thought we had 37 total, however..." trailing off, she glanced at us over her shoulder. "Never mind." She resumed leading our trek to the office.

Waiting for us in the office was not just the principal, but also the school custodian, assistant principal and a uniformed police officer. At the sight of the badge, gun belt and bulletproof vest, Jamie instantly deflated.

Before anyone could speak though, Bronnie got in the first word. "Good morning Principal Duncan, Mr. Cort, Assistant Principal Nguyen and" she squinted at the police man's name tag, "Officer de la Rosa." She pronounced each name so fluently and carried on as an adult that the police officer even shook her hand. "Am I correct in assuming that you believe Jamie Caldwell is responsible for the vandalism to which Principal Duncan alluded during this morning announcements?"

Principal Duncan was the only person not confused by Bronnie's statement, so she responded. "Yes, Miss Browne. I assume you have some useful information to contribute to the matter?"

Bronnie evaded. "While I've not been briefed on the nature of the incident, I am, however, confident that Jamie was not the individual responsible and would like to offer a defense for him in this matter."

The officer snorted. "Just to clarify. You don't really know what happened, nor do you know those responsible. Yet, you are so sure that it was not this young man here," He gestured at me and I surreptitiously nodded my head towards Jamie. "That you took it upon yourself at the risk of punishment to support your friend."

I can tell you with absolute certainty that Jamie Caldwell and Bronnie

Browne are not friends. In fact, they probably had not spoken ten words to each other since school began, not in my presence anyway. It was probably because of this incorrect assumption that Bronnie hesitated, but then nodded. I figured that she figured that it would be faster just to agree rather than getting into a long and (mostly likely incomprehensible) explanation of why the hell she had volunteered for defense attorney duty.

The principal glared at Bronnie, who stared back at her undeterred.

"Come with us, you three." Mrs. Duncan finally announced.

By this point I supposed it was too late to assert that I had absolutely nothing to do with any of this and consequently kept my mouth tightly shut. My thoughts, however, strayed to what my new life in military school would be like. Surely a stunt like this would get us all expelled, and me sent somewhere I would have to clean latrines.

Bronnie merely strolled ahead of the adults, her head high, arms casually clasped behind her back. She might have even been singing.

We left the central building and followed the sidewalk to the first cottage.

Mr. Cort dug into his pockets and came out with a ring of keys fit for a dungeon master. Bronnie carefully observed the area around the building. She squatted, analyzed the grass and then inspected the windows of the cottage from where she stood and then questioned, no one in particular, "Has anyone searched the outside of the building?"

Mr. Cort shook his head and answered. "Not as far as I know. Mrs. Sheridon came out to get ready for her this morning ESL classes and saw the mess. She called me next thing."

"ESL?" Bronnie asked.

"English as a Second Language." Mrs. Duncan replied.

Bronnie acknowledged the answer with a bob of her head and kept up her inspection. Officer de la Rosa held his fist in front of his mouth to conceal a grin as he watched this young girl do his job for him. Principal Duncan seemed primed to object to the whole display, but just then Mr. Cort located the correct key and ushered us all in into the cottage.

When the announcement of vandalism had been made, I immediately imagined spray painted profanity, broken windows and perhaps the usual visual representation of male genitalia. Instead, there was a strong odor of something early and sweet, but beyond that, the scene was just your average looking classroom.

Eventually we came to see that the entire floor on the opposite side of the room along with the shelves all of the way up to the ceiling had been covered in a thick, brown substance. A dark liquid the color and consistency of molasses had oozed out of white five gallon buckets and dripped onto the linoleum floor, making "ploop" sounds as it landed. Specks of the stuff had splattered onto the ceiling tiles and the two closest rows of class desks, though the majority of the offending liquid seemed to be contained to just that half of the classroom.

The only other sign of disarray were black streaks on the linoleum floor between the open windows and the restroom, but those didn't look to be the same material as the ooze.

Bronnie inspected the room the abruptly turned to the adults. "Jamie Caldwell didn't do this."

The officer put his fist to his mouth and coughed. Mr. Cort stared at her in disbelief, and Principal Duncan was fuming.

"I'm sure you are very confident in your beliefs, Miss Browne, but we have security video evidence showing us just the opposite. He was seen entering this room last Saturday." Mrs. Duncan she wrung her hands.

Bronnie dismissed the statement with a flick of her wrist. "That may be true, but doesn't necessarily represent what actually happened in this room." She ignored the seething school employee and wandered toward the bathroom being careful not to tread on the black streaks. "Am I to assume that the vandalism that occurred has to do with the..." she sniffed the air, "...with the root beer spillage and nothing else? No other damage?"

Mr. Cort shifted his stand and mumbled. "That and these confounded black streaks all over my nice white linoleum. Marking soles shouldn't be allowed on school premises. Takes me hours to get my floors clean again. No respect for the time..." he trailed off.

Mrs. Duncan ignored the janitor and went toe to toe with the curly haired detective. "Yes, that was the only damage. And there was no one else seen coming into or going out of this building on the security system the rest of the weekend. We checked. Jamie was seen entering through that window" she gestured to the near wall "carrying a large duffel. The bag most likely had the root beer in it. We had to conclude it was him who made this mess."

"No, you didn't have to conclude it was Jamie." Bronnie shrugged and turned away, undaunted by the challenge.

"Listen to me, young lady. I know you are new to this school, maybe even to this country, but we expect our students to conduct themselves with some respect. If you do not have anything useful to add, other than snide remarks, I suggest you go back to your class and leave the authorities to deal with Mr. Caldwell."

My friend's fist clenched and then relaxed.

Jamie finally spoke, maybe now more in Bronnie's defense than his own. "But she is right, I didn't do anything. I just came in to hide."

Officer de la Rosa tilted his head to look Jamie in the eye with a careful and gentle gaze, "Hide from what?"

Jamie took a deep breath. "I was hiding from Hector. His crew and him, they were chasing after me because I accidentally hit him in the head with a soccer ball."

"Hector Spector" was the official nickname given to the school bully, whom I had originally dubbed "Pokey-finger". Unfortunately, the less intimidating moniker wasn't the one that stuck. Probably because it didn't rhyme. Sometimes it is all in the marketing.

Mr. Cort raised his eyebrows, wanting Jamie to go on, but his bravery had run its course.

Bronnie gathered herself and walked back to the window facing the school, the one that would have appeared on the security video. "Last Saturday the school pitch was home to the usual football, sorry, I mean soccer, matches. Jamie, while fleeing from Hector, saw this window had been left slightly ajar, opened it and climbed into the classroom." She pointed to black streaks on the floor that ran from the open window to the coat closet on the far side of the room. "You can see the scuff marks from Jamie's soccer boots that he ran directly over to the other side of the room and hid in the loo." She stated, gesturing to the restroom.

Officer de la Rosa nodded, "That seems plausible. So tell me then, what about all of this soda?"

Bronnie pointed to three large white buckets that sat on the highest wall shelf, above eye level for the adults, where most of the sticky sludge was still dripping down. The tops of the buckets almost reached the low ceiling. "If you retrieve those containers, you will see that they have root beer still in them."

Mr. Cort shifted some desks, stood on a chair and began to get the buckets down. "It sure smells like root beer. Makes me wish I had some vanilla ice cream." He quipped.

Mrs. Duncan rolled her eyes in defeat. "Ok, Miss Browne. You were right that it was root beer, but how do you know Jamie was not the one responsible."

Bronnie gave me the smallest of grins. "Sean, do you remember what we did in Mr. Blenheim's advanced science class last week."

"Sure," I said, "Chemistry."

"Not much help, Sean." Bronnie indicated the buckets. "This isn't just any root beer; this is homemade. Which is concocted when you mix flavoring ingredients with yeast, water, and various kinds of sugar. Then it is left to ferment which will create natural carbonation."

Jamie stared at her blankly.

"It makes it fizzy." She translated for him.

"So Mr. Blenheim came in here last week, my guess would be Thursday, after having mixed the ingredients and placed them in the containers. He placed the buckets on the shelf. But it would appear he either added too much yeast or the room was too warm, or both. The mixture fermented quickly," she inspected lid in her hands, turning it over, " and they did not use the correct lids for brewing which contain valves in order to allow fermentation gasses to escape. The containers would have burst open with some force, depositing some of the liquid on the ceiling and desks. The remainder would have flowed out of the containers, onto the shelves and floor." She placed the lid back on the bucket and wiped her hands on a handkerchief she pulled from her jeans pocket.

Officer de la Rosa jotted something down in a small black notebook, "How do you know it wasn't a student who did this?"

"Besides the general assumption that a student probably wouldn't think to make root beer from scratch in a school's special use classroom?"

"Besides that." He conceded.

She reseated her headband and gazed at the shelves. "Judging by the amount of soda on the shelves and ground, those buckets had to be nearly full. A five-gallon bucket full of water would weigh over forty pounds."

"Are you sure?" Officer de la Rosa baited.

"Absolutely. A gallon of water weighs 8.34 pounds. The additional sugar in the root beer would raise its density, and therefore it's weight, even more. No offense, Jamie, but I don't see you having the ability to strict-press almost fifty pounds directly over your head while standing on a chair."

"No offense taken." Jamie replied and then visibly relaxed.

Bronnie was about to speak again but was interrupted by Mrs. Duncan. "The three of you may return to class."

Chapter 4

Mr. Cort confirmed with Mr. Blenheim
that he had, in fact, brought in supplies
to make root beer. Also, having
retrieved the recipe from the Internet
he couldn't be sure the recipe ratios
were correct. So Bronnie and I found
ourselves sitting at lunch with a third
person that day, a very grateful Jamie
Caldwell.

A week or so later, on a Friday, our
teacher took the familiar top hat off of
her desk and held it out. Her same
retro glasses and a bright cherry print
dress with a pouffy skirt made her

appear straight out of an I Love Lucy episode.

"My Minions, guess what time it is." She sang.

"Lunch time!" one of the smart-ass kids from the back of the class yelled in reply.

Mrs. Andrews laughed. "You wish. No, my friends, it is science project time! So if the left side of the class would kindly come up and pick a name from the hat, that would be fabulous."

Amidst the almost universal groans, my side of the class rose and wandered reluctantly to the front. Even though my desk was in the middle rows, somehow I managed to find myself further and further from the top hat.

Then, when I was the last person at the front of the room, Mrs. Andrews shifted the hat to her other hand and leaned it over towards me. "This last one is for you, Mr. Watkins." She confided.

I reached into the hat but somehow already knew whose name would be on the small slip of paper.

The following afternoon, I hopped on Mr. Jenkins, my skateboard, and made my way to Bronnie's house. Mr. Jenkins is what I named my newest skateboard after a drugstore clerk in West Virginia (who was convinced I would rob him or graffiti his store every time I rode by) confiscated my old one.

Rather than argue with him or the authorities about the ancient board, my mom decided buying a new badass version was a much better form of revenge. I named the new board after that jerk and even had a friend laminate a caricature of him to the deck as one last parting shot.

Mother Nature had finally gotten the memo that a change of seasons was in order, much to my disappointment. She was currently hating on me with a nipping light rain just slightly too warm to be snow.

"This weather sucks!" I observed on my way out the door.

"Suck it up, buttercup!" Mom yelled back. Perhaps if she had not been in the military, she would have been a tad more sympathetic.

Two years in the mountains had given me enough time to learn to enjoy snow, but this freezing rain crap was something else entirely. If this weird mix was all this New England peninsula had to offer for winter, I might start lobbying to move again.

By the time I rolled the half-mile to Bronnie's classic New England style home even my bones were frozen. It was covered in pale yellow clapboard siding and a dark gray slate roof. A white picket fence and what were probably rose bushes rimming the yard. The roses were nothing stumps of thorny, leafless twigs now since they had been trimmed back for the winter.

Probably it had started out as a modest, two-story cottage then over the years started to ramble like a drunken uncle at Thanksgiving. There were two front doors and two paths leading to them from the sidewalk. As my plan of attack, I chose the one on the left leading to what appeared to be the more formal side of the house. This side probably had been the original home being build by Captain Gorton in 1834, or so the brass nameplate at eye level would have be believe. Seeing no button for a doorbell around the mass of wood trim, I grasped the green ring beard of a Gandalf looking door knocker and gave it a good clang.

No one seemed to have heard. I glanced around the corner to the right of the door, wondering if I had made the correct choice. The second footpath went on for about twenty more feet into the yard, leading to the full porch and a more common screened door combo. Two dormer windows on the second floor peeked out of the roof.

Clanging Gandalf's face again, my thoughts wandered to what Bronnie's family might be like. In my imagination, it had run the gamut from college professors in tweed jackets to superheroes, to assassins and then back again. Finally I heard soft creaking of wood on the other side of the wall.

The front door began to open then stopped, I heard someone mutter a Level One curse on the other side followed by a soft grunt. The door jolted again and swung open with a groan of old wood and rusty hinges. A lovely woman with skin almost the same color as Bronnie's beamed at me. She was striking, delicate and probably weighed barely a hundred pounds. Her dark hair peeked out from under a rose scarf that complemented a green and rose tunic.

"Oh hello! You must be Sean. Please, please, do come in out of this weather." She heaved the door closed behind me, "This door sticks terribly when it rains. This way" she padded down the hall in embroidered slippers. "I was just putting the kettle on. Bronnie will be down any moment."

She was quick, halfway down the hall before I could respond. I chased after her down the length of the original house, past a staircase and an enormous grandfather clock that tick-tocked along happily in the foyer.

"That big old thing came with the house." She gestured to the clock. "It makes the most awful racket every hour, but we haven't had the heart to stop the chimes."

We strode passed a living room and dining room, complete with weird colonial wallpaper and a grand piano. Finally we turned a corner and ended up in the kitchen at the back of the house. Mrs. Browne gestured for me to sit on a barstool near the counter and immediately turned to pull a tray of cookies out of the oven.

Never one to resist a swivel chair, I spun about on the barstool as the kettle began to whistle. With my back to the counter, I noticed that the porch door at the front of the house led to the kitchen. Somewhere in the depths of another part of the house I heard a rhythmic clunking sound.

"You are more than welcome to use the porch from now on, Sean."

She was observant, like her daughter.

Mrs. Browne continued. "Now I'm accustomed to making things such as scones and almond biscuits, however, I'm told that the sweet of choice in the states is the chocolate chip version?" She grinned and passed a china plate to me with one of each option.

"Wow! They all look great." And then I gorged probably more than was socially acceptable.

"Glad you like them. Would you like tea or milk?" As if to pre-empt any argument, she presented both options on a tray.

Munching on my cookie, I perused the local newspaper, which had been left on the counter. Someone had left it open to an article written about our school field hockey team. One curly haired girl, in the background and not given a name in the subtitle, had been circled with a pencil. It reminded me that I probably needed to start getting in shape for the upcoming soccer season, since I'd chosen to bail on fall and winter sports.

There was an exasperated sigh from my right. "Mother," Bronnie said as she thunked onto the landing of a corner staircase I had not noticed.

Her mom's smile faded faintly. "What, love? Am I not allowed to offer your classmate some refreshment? He did venture here on his skateboard, after all. And it is raining if you hadn't noticed."

"This precipitation hardly qualifies as rain. And making three different kinds of cookies is rather overkill." Bronnie countered.

I couldn't tell if this was a play argument or the beginnings of a real one.

"What are guests for if not to spoil?" Shrugging at her daughter, she turned off the oven, slid her laptop off the counter and left for the living room. "Enjoy your project. Leave the door open!" She called over her shoulder.

Bronnie rolled her eyes so hard I could almost hear them. She motioned for me to follow her back up the stairs. I held the plate of cookies up in question and began to plead with my best puppy dog eyes.

"Fine, bring those too." She said and as a last minute thought, snagged chocolate chip of her own off the cooling rack before leading me up the back stairs.

At the landing, another section of house veered off towards the back of the lot. The room leading to it was so dark it was indistinguishable. She yelled into the blackness, "Da! What is that infernal banging? Do you have nunchucks in the clothes dryer?"

A man's smooth and deep voice replied. "Absolutely not. You know I air-dry my nunchucks."

I snorted.

Bronnie glared at no one in particular, then nudged me. "Be very careful up these stairs. They are worn down and have been painted, and so are very slippery."

I gripped the railing well and worked my way up what felt more like a ladder on a sailboat.

"And don't bump your head!" Bronnie cautioned just in time to hear me clunk my noggin on the sloped ceiling. "Sorry." She offered.

"It's cool." I said, massaging the spot, "Didn't hit too hard."

Looking around for a place to sit, I noticed a double bed between the dormer windows, a dresser, a bookcase and an old wing-backed chair stacked with books. Not wanting to go near the bed and seeing no other furniture in a room almost thirty feet long, I opted to stand there like an idiot rubbing my head with one hand and holding the plate of cookies in the other.

If Bronnie didn't have much in the way of furniture, she made up for it with stuff. Outside of my packrat great-grandmother's house, I'd never seen such a random assortment of junk in my life. The floors were stacked with books. The bookshelf was littered with things like non-matching china teacups, opera glasses, harmonicas, and classic video game cartridges.

A pile of shoes (many far too big to be Bronnie's) was shoved into the corner. Neatly stacked all over the room were colorful subscription mailing boxes containing who knows what.

There was also a disconcerting assortment of weapons including a fencing sword, a compound archery bow, and a medieval-looking device that was a leather wrapped stick with two spiked metal balls attached by chains. She also owned funky looking guitar, some kind of brass horn and a violin. I noticed the corners of the ceiling held small mirrors, but from my angle I couldn't tell what they should be showing me.

Bronnie heaved the books to the floor and perched herself cross-legged on the wing chair, she pointed to a door I had overlooked on her left at the opposite end of the room. "That is the loo if you need it." She took a bite of her cookie and gestured with her thumb to a door behind her. "That leads to the other end of the house."

Raising my eyebrows, "And this door?" I said, nodding towards my right.

"Ah, now that..." She got up, "is the entrance to my secret lair."

She definitely seemed like the kind of person to have a secret lair.

Bronnie turned a lever, which moved a long arm, which spun a gear, which moved another gear. A few more things happened in the chain of events making this the most elaborate doorknob I had ever seen. The louvered door creaked open, and an overhead light automatically turned on to illuminate a long walk-in closet. Clothes hung neatly on the rod closest to the door, protected from the world by a clear wardrobe cover. That was pretty much where the usual closet contents ended.

Bronnie slid by me and sat on a swivel desk chair then pushed another stool belonging to the drafting table towards me. "It isn't much, but it is private. Most of my more interesting tools are in the workshop. Mum doesn't like me working with heat or chemicals where we have carpeting."

"Probably smart." I ventured while eating the scone, which was determined to leave a trail of breadcrumbs throughout the house.

Wedged into the small space was the drafting table where I sat with rulers and angles, erasers and pencils. There was her desk which held microscope with accompanying vials and slides as well as laptop on a vertical stand, as well as a two computer monitors. One monitor was running a series of green and red numbers, like stock market tickers.

The other monitor had four tiles social media websites open, with photos of students and teachers tiled across the desktop. The largest tile was a calendar update for the Graphic Design and Photographic Arts club at school run by Miss Faraday.

Posters of the periodic table, constellations, and a map of the London Underground plastered the sloped ceiling. The rear wall had another small bookcase holding textbooks and leather bound novels of some kind. On top of the shelf was an open box full of sewing supplies, random wires, and electronics. She had an organizer with what looked like a hundred different kinds of nail polish, which I found conspicuous because I'd never seen Bronnie wear nail polish.

And lastly, there was a glass mason jar with a bizarre looking rodent floating in a yellow liquid.

So gross. Not gross enough, however, to make me stop eating cookies.

Above the shelf on a cork board were printed lists of numbers and a map of the United States. Brightly colored pushpins were stuck into the map and connected to the printouts with yarn.

We sat in silence and stared at each other for what must have been a few minutes.

"Right, the science project!" I suddenly declared. "What do you want to do?"

She shrugged, her hand toying with a blue rubber wristwatch lying on her desk. It occurred to me now, looking around, that something as pedestrian as making a model of the solar system would not be an option. In fact, like there was probably not a single project that I could come up with she hadn't already tested, in preschool.

For being pretty good friends at school, we were both extremely awkwardly in her weird little lair. I tapped the ruler on the drafting table. "So you obviously do some experimenting in your spare time. What kinds of research do you like to do?"

"Bit of this, bit of that. I've played with the Briggs-Rauscher reaction, done some work with explosive powers of mercury fulminate, observed the rate at which different tissues decompose." She mused. "They are nothing ground-breaking, but I find it helps the learning process to get one's hands dirty."

"Yep, no solar system for us." I whispered, looking around desperately. "Is that your watch?" I asked, pointing towards her hand.

"This? No." She flipped it so I could see that there was no watch face where one would be, just a flat black disc. "It is a **GPS** tracker."

"What for?" I scooted my stool closer.

"It was mine, for a while." She handed it over to me.

My eyes opened wide in amazement. "Your parents track you?"

"They got it when I was younger, apparently I was a bolter." Swinging her chair around from one side to the other, not having enough room in the closet to turn fully around.

"Oh." I replied, "We'll probably need something like that when Margot gets older."

"Is she an independent spirit?"

"You could say that. She is definitely the youngest and knows how to play us already." My eyes surveyed the room again, careful to steer clear of the weird yellow jar. I pointed to the map and yarn. "What's all that about?"

Bronnie swiveled her chair to face it. "That's just a pet project of mine."

"Aaaaand?" I urged.

She gazed at it thoughtfully. "I'm attempting to discover if there is one specific triggering factor which lead to local socioeconomic rebirths."

Gesturing to the map."

I must have appeared dumbfounded because she took one glance at me and kept talking.

"Those pins represent specific locations of depressed neighborhoods that have experienced an unusual economic revival in the last 15 years. I suppose the representation is somewhat superfluous because I'm looking at towns or zip codes and that map is far too large to give any detail. But it was lying around, and I like the visual aid. It helps."

I stood up to get a better look at the map. "Helps what?"

"Helps connect the random thoughts in my head, somehow, I'm not sure how."

There were points marked in New Orleans, Detroit, Indianapolis, Georgia, even the area where I had lived in West Virginia seemed to be highlighted. "Did you find out what they are? The factors I mean?"

Bronnie stood next to me. For some reason I noticed she smelled like watermelon. "Not yet. I'm far from finished. On a large scale, factors such as tax incentives for businesses, a population's access to higher education or the presence of a skilled workforce can influence the strength of an economy. However, on the micro level, perhaps for a small town or a neighborhood, my hypothesis centers on restaurants. I think a single great place to eat can change an entire town."

"Really?" I encouraged, only faking it a little bit.

She beamed. "Of course it isn't so simple as just a restaurant. A local renaissance has to be done properly. You need walkable landscape that encourage people to stay longer in the area and assist neighboring businesses. A picturesque location will also draw tourists or romantics. But people, as a rule, will endure almost anything and go almost anywhere for really great food. Now that you Yanks have discovered quality over quantity, it is happening even more."

She pointed her small finger at a red pushpin on the coast of Georgia. "We stopped here over the summer, on our way back from Florida. A little restaurant was in an old part of what had been a busy port town. The building was surrounded by empty warehouses and dilapidated houses. However, restaurant itself was jammed and the parking lot chock full of expensive cars. As we left I noticed someone had recently bought an old warehouse across the street and was turning it into modern loft apartments. Coffee shops and art galleries were set to open on the next block. It made me wonder if the little restaurant, surviving in a forgotten town, had been what began the rebirth."

She looked at her work on the wall as if it were one whole picture, not a bunch of different pins and maps and numbers. "Restaurants are expensive to open." She continued. "Great chefs who want to take risks usually don't have financial backers, which means they need cheap buildings. So they seek out forgotten neighborhoods and small towns."

I pointed to the pin in West Virginia. "Which restaurant is here?"

"Ah, there are a few possibilities there, but I think the one that tipped the scale is called Stardust." She mused.

"I've been there."

"Truly? Is that is where you lived?"

"Sort of close." I said. "Dad went to the medical school there, but mom had a job further away, so we kind of lived in between the two. I lived for the sticky toffee pudding."

She laughed. "You realize that is a traditional British dessert."

"I'm surprised it was so good then." I joked.

She hit me on the shoulder and then began to pepper me with questions about the town and surrounding area. Most of which I couldn't answer since they were about population density, property values, and tax rates. I did manage to remember recent openings of a concert hall and a big fitness center, which appeased her somewhat.

"So are you finished with your project?" I asked.

She shook her head. "Oh no. I have much more work to do. Right now the numbers support my hypothesis. I don't want to jump to a conclusion. Another factor could cause these revivals, one I haven't found yet, so I'm far from finished." She took out a lollipop and became thoughtful. "I suppose that is what I don't like about the scientific method."

"Huh?" I blurted, wondering what turn in the conversation I missed.

"It seems to me that the scientific method is deductive reasoning. It is the act of forming a hypothesis is jumping to the conclusion and then proceeding to search for the proof." She handed me a lollipop from a jar full of them. "I prefer the method of *induction* more to *deduction*. Following the proof to find the hypothesis, the cause, if you will. Then again, if you have a hypothesis at all, I suppose it means you have already done some research. Still, it seems like putting the cart before the horse."

My forehead wrinkled, I couldn't tell if she was talking to herself or me.

She turned abruptly and cocked her head to one side, "Why do you always wear that cap?"

There was a knock at the door and I flinched. Bronnie didn't move.

"Yes, mum?" She said.

Her mom took a step inside the closet. "Just checking, love." She smiled at me warmly, "May I get you anything? Another cookie? Cuppa tea? Drop you off in the middle of nowhere and let you find your way home?"

"My mom would like you." I chuckled.

Bronnie interjected. "Does she have an embarrassing sense of humor as well?"

"For sure. Probably even worse." I responded dryly.

"Love to meet her." Mrs. Browne grinned.

Bronnie was trying hard stare her out of the closet but her mother was deftly ignoring the effort.

Finally, I said, "I would love a cup of tea, ma'am. If it isn't too much trouble."

Mrs. Browne touched me lightly on the arm, "No trouble at all." She nodded her head ever so slightly towards her daughter and ducked out of the room.

"Your mom is nice," I said but didn't get a response.

Bronnie turned to face her cork board on the wall. "So, the cap," she pointed to my head, "you always seem to wear it."

"Oh, this?" I removed the knit beanie, suddenly feeling self-conscious. "Yeah, I guess so."

"You know, it is impolite to wear a hat indoors." She hinted to me.

"Force of habit," I replied. "I have crazy hair." I couldn't tell if she was upset or not. My guess was not, but still, I twisted the beanie in my hands then tossed it on the drafting table next to my cell phone.

Bronnie shrugged. "It suits you, your surfer look."

I grinned, stupidly I'm sure.

"I'm going to use the bathroom," I said and crept out of the awkward moment. As I passed Bronnie's wing-backed chair, I chanced to see a mirror on the shelf next to it and was startled to see her mom's image in it; she was beginning to walk up the stairs while holding a tea tray. Her mother moved out of the frame and then at the landing a few seconds later.

"Ah." she said, "I see you've found Bronwyn's security system."

"Surveillance system!" Bronnie corrected from within the closet.

Mrs. Browne rolled her eyes. "Yes, surveillance. The security system would be the array of weaponry littered throughout the room."

"That is stretching it, don't you think?" Bronnie bellowed.

"It is not polite to raise your voice. If you would like to join our conversation, please come out of your lair." Her mother retorted.

Her daughter replied with a "Humph", but didn't come out.

Mrs. Browne searched the room and decided to place the tray on the chair. "Good luck!" She called and left the room by the side door, not the stairs.

Before finally using the restroom, I inspected it for more surveillance mirrors, cameras, bugs or any random spy gear that might be hidden. I also checked behind the shower curtain, because that is what you do in a strange bathroom. Looking at my reflection in the, presumably unmonitored, vanity mirror, I cursed Bronnie making me take off my hat and tried to use my wet hands to straighten my hat hair. It didn't do much good.

When I got back, Bronnie had my beanie in her hands. She looked up at me. "What does this signify?" She asked, pointing to the patch on my beanie.

"Oh, that is just a surf company logo. The beanie was my dad's, but he said I could have it since my head is so big."

She looked at me thoughtfully. I did a mental face palm.

"How about I help you with the map," I said finally. "For our project."

"Which map?" She responded.

"You have more than one?"

"I have many." She replied again. Then her gaze followed mine to the cork board on the wall. "Oh, that map."

It wasn't exactly my idea of a fun science project, but it was all I could think of. If we hadn't come up with a topic soon, we would probably have spent another hour staring at each other in this closet.

"Right. Fine. Unless something better comes along." She took the cork board off of the wall. "Grab my laptop, if you would. We can work downstairs where there is more space."

We set up shop at the round kitchen table, I went back for the tea tray. The sugar rush was welcome because Bronnie set me up with a list of towns and their corresponding property tax, sales tax and population data for the past 15 years. All the while she kept mumbling to herself about "30-second intervals" and "global positioning reliability." I mostly tuned her out and nodded when it seemed appropriate.

My eyes were nearly glazed over from scrutinizing spreadsheets when Mrs. Browne suddenly announced that the sun was beginning to set. She invited me to have dinner with them. I pulled out my phone and noticed six unread texts from my parents. They were probably livid, so it was my cue to go home. Bronnie walked me to the door, straightened the beanie on my head, punched me lightly on the arm and said goodbye.

Girls are weird.

I texted Bronnie in the morning to see if there was any work I could do for our project in an attempt to be helpful but really hoping for a free pass. She gave me some more maps and addresses to plot then asked if I would be home all day or if we had any plans.

The next few days were like that. I would get quite a few texts from

Bronnie asking where I was, what my plans were, as though she were hoping for an invitation.

My dad began to wonder if Bronnie had become my girlfriend. Thankful that most of my upcoming commitments involved family it gave me a great excuse not to invite her along. She must have felt slighted, because at school, Bronnie would glance at me, write in her notebook, and then look away again.

After almost two weeks of creepy stalker behavior she bounded up to me, positively giddy. "Sean, are you free tomorrow afternoon?"

I thought about her straightening my hat, punching me in the arm, texting me all of the time. Did she think we were dating? It may have been this feeling that led my first answer to sound more rude than I intended.

"Why?" I snapped.

She clasped her hands together and swung them happily, "For our science project. We are nearly finished."

I tried to think of a good excuse to bail but couldn't. "OK, I can be over around 2." We did need to finish the project and, if she did have other ideas about our relationship, we'd have the privacy of her creepy closet for me to set her straight. Better to end it there than in the middle of the school where she might embarrass me.

The next day, I rode on my board through a thick fog, which left drops of water on my clothes and face. The fall weather had stayed damp, wet and downright dismal. The locals cheerfully assured me that winter would be much the same and not worry. Rarely did they get snow they couldn't sweep.

Great. Cold, damp and not even a glimmer of hope for snow days.

This time I hopped up to the front porch of Bronnie's house instead banging Galdalf's head on the groaning door. While waiting for someone to answer, I noticed an old-fashioned mail slot in the door and a small mirror mounted in the corner of the porch ceiling in front of me. I waved to it.

Bronnie swung the door open without her usual reserve. She was a breathless mess and almost unrecognizable in sweaty workout clothes, leather fingerless gloves and a bandana holding back her curls. "You are late." She accused.

"Soccer game ran over." I lied, as I leaned my Mr. Jenkins against the porch wall and slid through.

"You are a terrible liar." She waved for me to follow her up the stairs.

I hesitated near the kitchen in hopes of cookies, but it didn't appear like I would get any. Mrs. Browne's voice was coming from the dining room with the same tone my mother gets during work calls. From the sounds of her footsteps and the fading and rise of the volume, she was pacing like my mom did too.

"What are you wearing?" I managed to ask as Bronnie took the stairs two at a time.

She glanced down. "Exercise gear, dad and I were lifting." She said.

"Lifting what?"

"Weights, silly. Speed and power are not mutually exclusive." She declared and practically launched herself into the closet.

"TA-DA!" she cheered, using her arms to show off a map on the wall like a game show model might.

It was just her same map of cities marked with pins and then connected by yarn. "Uh huh, yeah. Good job." I asked, playing along and very relieved that she didn't try to kiss me.

She seemed deflated. "What do you think? I finished it." She urged, "Just today. Put the last pin in about an hour ago."

Stepping closer to the map, I realized it wasn't the same one I had seen two weeks before. It wasn't a map of the country at all, but one of our New England county complete with color-coded pins and matching yarn, some pink, some orange, some green. It also contained handwritten date and time stamps next to each pin with coordinated list printouts and even a few surveillance photos taped around the sides.

My head got light and the room started to tilt to one side. This might have looked like an **FBI** surveillance workup if I hadn't known better.

"Oh my god Bronnie. Is this? What is this?" I stammered.

"It is you!" She gushed. "All of your movements for a fortnight. Well, most of them. You can imagine there was a fair amount of overlap!"

She was elated.

I was speechless.

"I was so excited to finally have a test subject for the experiment I'd wanted to try! What better time to do it than for the school science project. Of course, I've tried to do this sort of thing before with stray dogs in the neighborhood and even once with my mum, but they weren't very cooperative."

"You tracked me?" I managed to speak finally, but she wasn't listening.

"Of course. I couldn't test the accuracy of the global positioning device unless I could also independently verify that the subject's exact location. And one can hardly expect a stray dog to reply to text messages. My mother is not exactly an ideal test subject either. But you were PERFECT Sean! An absolutely perfect test subject. Except for the one time when you said you were at the library and you were clearly at the skate park."

"You tracked me..." I whispered.

"Yes. Focus Sean! So my goal was to test two different GPS systems against one another. I didn't want to add a tracker app to your mobile phone and complicate that method, so I needed ping your phone manually for location updates."

She inhaled deeply. "Whereas my kid tracker **GPS** program sends me updates every 30 seconds, I had to manually ping your mobile phone for comparison. It was definitely more labor intensive. But, at least we had two software applications on two separate wireless devices, on the same mobile network to compare. After compiling over two weeks worth of data and there was finally enough to come to a reasonable conclusion."

There was a definite part of me that wanted to vomit.

"While the telephone tracker was accurate 70% of the time," she continued, "there were some significant glitches. Occasionally the location given was off by as much as two miles. I think we can reasonably conclude that the **GPS** tracker, given its more advanced software and it's rapid refresh rate, is the more accurate of the two systems." She was so excited, so proud.

So oblivious.

"You tracked me and didn't tell me?" I managed to squeak out. I was finding difficult, however, to continue to be angry with someone who had absolutely no clue that they had done anything wrong.

Bronnie pulled two lollipops out of her pocket and handed me one. "Hawthorne effect." She said.

Like I knew what that was.

I held onto the candy but didn't open the wrapper. The map and accompanying printout logged my trips to school, the ice cream shop, my dad's office, the skate park (library), even the cold and windy little boat trip we took across the sound to an even colder and windier picnic on an island barely the size of a soccer field.

She shifted the lollipop to her cheek like a squirrel. Her tone had changed, it was almost apologetic. "The Hawthorne effect states that most subjects will alter their behavior, no matter what that behavior is, if they think they are being observed."

She took my phone from my hand, logged into it with my six digit passcode and removed the permission to track my location from her profile.

"May I have your cap?"

I handed it over with a shrug and then slumped onto the floor. She perched on her office chair, took some sewing items from a tackle box and went to work on the underside of the logo patch on my beanie.

"Not to mention the observer-expectancy effect. I mean, it was bad enough having to text you all of the time to get your location verified. Any more and I might have begun to influence your movements." She mumbled with the candy still in her cheek. "Perhaps that is why you said you were at the library instead of skateboarding."

She took a small hook and used it to cut stitches from the edge of the patch and then removed the black disc tracker, which had been in the blue watchband not two weeks before.

Clever.

And creepy.

She tossed the disk on the desk and set to work sewing the section of patch back on to my hat. "See, my mom takes her phone everywhere, every day, but nothing else stays the same. She never wears the same clothes, takes the same purse, or even the same car. She is not a creature of habit. I think our mothers are alike in that way. And stray dogs, well, you could never expect a dog to text you back with their accurate location." Knotting the last stitch, she tore the thread with her teeth and held it up to me. "There, good as new!"

I started to laugh. It began as a chuckle and turned into a full-fledged howl.

The triumphant look on her face changed to confusion. "What is so funny?"

"I can't believe you've been tracking me for two weeks for our science project." I kept laughing, and my eyes started to water. "All of this time," pausing to catch my breath, "all this time I thought you were crushing on me."

Bronnie's face became serious, "Pardon me?"

Her response made it even funnier. I tried to explain between laughs and gasps for air.

"All of those texts asking where I was, what I was doing. I thought, that you thought, that we were dating."

She stared at me blankly for a beat, blinked and finally replied. "Wow, if I were a lesser person I might find your humor at the proposition insulting." And with that tossed me my beanie.

Insert a few moments of uncomfortable silence here.

"So," I said, finally catching my breath and trying to lighten the mood, "Since you aren't looking to date me and you aren't, presumably, spying on me anymore, want to go down to Dave's shop and get some ice cream?"

She stood up quickly. "Sounds lovely."

"Wait." I said at the door. "What the hell was I working on the last two weeks if it wasn't our science project?"

Bronnie scooted past me and mumbled "I suppose I'm buying."

Later that week, after we had presented our project to a stupefied class, Mrs. Andrews pulled me aside after the bell for lunch.

"That was excellent work that you and Bronnie did, Sean. I am proud of both of you." She said while stacking some papers on the desk.

"Mrs. Andrews, you paired us on purpose, didn't you?"

She pretended she hadn't heard me.

"The day with the top hat, when everyone drew names. You avoided me long enough to have me go last, so you could make sure I got Bronnie's name."

Her grin seemed forced. "Bronnie is a brilliant person, Sean, though her grades may not always show it. Sometimes she needs help in certain areas, like a partner. Someone who understands her and won't get frustrated."

I'd like to meet the person who wouldn't get frustrated with Bronnie.

Mrs. Andrews removed her black-rimmed glasses, showing a gentle look in her eyes. "She responds to you Sean and you seem to get along well with her. I'm not saying you have to be best friends, but you do appear to make a good team."

"Can you imagine if you had paired Blaire with her? All designer shoes and nail polish." I mused.

"Or Jamie? He would have been stunned silent for two weeks." She chuckled and sighed. "Come on. I'll walk with you to the cafeteria. And to answer your question, yes, I did rig the drawing."

"I understand."

Mrs. Andrews nodded. "Just one question, Sean."

"Fire away." I answered, instinctively counting the number of art projects on the walls as we went.

"Did Bronnie tell you she that she would be tracking your movements the whole two weeks?" She inquired, a sly grin forming as she spoke.

"Of course not," I responded with the most Bronnie-esque voice I could muster. "As the Hawthorne Effect states, that kind of forewarning clearly could have influenced the integrity of the experiment."

She laughed for real this time, and I held the door to the cafeteria open for her.

Interlude:
January 22, 2011

Running away from one troublesome man had left my daughter and me prey to others. Simply removing the one decent thing my ex-husband had given us, some financial security, I was now back to work out in the world. For a woman who had never gone to college and went right to being a mom, it meant barely living above minimum wage.

Which also meant we were living in questionable neighborhoods. In general we had very sweet neighbors, but there was also always an undercurrent of trouble. Gangs were more common in these areas, but also petty robberies, catcalls, you name it. All of these unsavories figured folks in these neighborhoods either didn't trust the police enough to call or weren't worth the uniform's time.

In bigger cities it was easier to disappear from my ex, but it also meant I was invisible to most everyone else who as well.

Then, right when things were looking up, I had done the unthinkable. I'd set up a home phone in my name, my maiden name. Three weeks later, there he was waiting for me in the parking lot after my shift at the diner. A statue of seething rage, his arms were crossed as he leaned against what he presumed to be my car.

We used to play a game at the shelter that worked in tandem with our self defense classes. We moms would try to startle one another, to scare each other constantly. The goal was to build up a tolerance to being surprised so that, if one day our exes found us again we could act without hesitation.

He launched himself off of the car, uncrossed his arms and came at me fast while balling his fists.

My hand had already been in my purse reaching for my keys, but as he moved towards me I came up with can of pepper spray instead. It was something I purchased at a camping store and really was meant for taking down grizzly bears. I stood upwind hosed my own predator with the stuff from fifteen feet away.

He went down like the only kid on a seesaw.

Chapter 5

Requisite turkey decorations in their usual brown and orange hues plastered around the school soon gave way to paper snowflakes, ornaments, and pictures of the younger grades with Santa hats on their heads. Every bit of wall not festooned with the fruits of school's artist inspiration held reminders for the upcoming winter concert.

The weekend after Thanksgiving was incredibly crowded, worse than I had ever seen it. Families and local businesses had set up booths in the gymnasium, selling things like doll clothes, jewelry and cupcakes to raise money for the school PTA. The halls displayed raffle baskets and artwork for sale from the upper grades. While it made for a festive and fun atmosphere, the school was almost impossible to navigate.

Bronnie and I were going in search of someplace to get a snack before the concert when we heard a cry.

We turned to see a young girl taking up what little free space there was with her blubbering form while she pointed at the wall with her little shaky finger. Her mother was attempting to comfort her. Bronnie and I pushed our way forward through the crowd around her, but instead of going passed, my friend stopped.

It turned out we knew her. Her name was Cherie and she was the little sister of a classmate. Bronnie looked at Cherie, then the wall, then back at her.

"What is the matter?" Bronnie asked somewhat rhetorically.

Cherie was so upset, she couldn't speak, her breath kept getting caught in her throat. Her mom was smoothing her hair, but she turned to answer Bronnie. "Her picture she did in art class is gone. Someone tore it off of the wall." She spoke kindly, but rolled her eyes in apology for the scene her kid was making.

Bronnie scrutinized the wall. Middle grade classes had been given the project envisioning a replacement for Santa's eight flying reindeer. On the wall, two long rows of pictures displayed various sleighs being pulled by mice, fairies, robotic caribou, flying squirrels (mine) and a giant Ford Mustang Convertible (Bronnie's).

But on the bottom row, smack dab in the middle, two pieces of artwork were missing. Everything was gone except one small bit of red construction paper and a piece of tape from what would have been the top left corner of the picture that had been on the left.

Bronnie pointed to the spot by that scrap of paper and said, "Was your picture here?"

By now, Cherie had calmed down enough to be able to talk, but she was hiccupping. "Yes. I painted it with my dog, Muffinhead, in the lead. I really wanted mom to see it."

I coughed to avoid a laugh. It is hard to keep a straight face when a name like Muffinhead gets thrown at you.

Twirling a curly lock of hair in thought, Bronnie scanned the rest of the pictures, and then asked no one in particular, "Whose picture was next to yours?"

Cherie rubbed her eyes, "I don't know."

Then quickly, as if she snapped out of a trance, Bronnie turned to her left and power walked through the crowds down the hall to the front of the school and cafeteria. She checked under tables and in open classrooms.

Finally, in a large trash can set in the hallway near the exit, she saw Cherie's picture. It was sitting on top of a pile of old coffee cups and paper towels but was otherwise undamaged.

Bronnie gingerly pulled it from the garbage, looked back into the can and then brought the rather terrible portrayal of a Pekinese pulling Santa's sleigh back to the little girl and her mother. Before she could say anything though Cherie practically tackled her in joy. Bronnie stared wideeyed from over the head of the young girl and reluctantly patted her on the back until she let go.

After accepting many thanks, not the least from Cherie's mom who was happy the melodramatic scene was over, we made our way towards the back of the school still in search of snacks. Finally, we found a bake sale table where I used my allowance for a giant chocolate cupcake that was sure to stain my white shirt. Bronnie bought two cookies and we found a quiet corner near the library where we could sit on the floor and eat.

She leaned in towards me, once we were comfortable, and said, "That was very strange."

"What?" I said, mouth half full of cupcake. "The thing with Cherie? Lots of kids drew pets pulling the sleigh. She did make a heck of a scene about it."

Bronnie shook her head, "No, not that. That isn't surprising at all actually." She took a bit of her cookie and chewed carefully for a moment. "There were 91 pictures on that wall."

I shrugged my shoulders. "Counting Cherie's or not?"

"Not." Bronnie said. "So if you count Cherie's and the other one that was missing, it makes 93."

"And that is strange because...?" I responded.

"There are only 92 kids in the mid grades, the grades that did that particular project." She said, and she turned to look back down the crowded hallway.

"Huh. Weird." I continued to eat my cupcake, completely missing the point.

She took a bite of cookie.

"Bronnie!" I called out the next day when I found her during free time. She was rubbing her arms to stay warm while sitting under the big ornamental strawberry tree with a notebook on her lap.

She looked up and then patted the spot of dirt next to her under the tree. She shivered and blew into her hands to warm them. The December wind coming off of the nearby water was biting cold. I instinctively moved a little closer to block the wind.

"Why aren't you wearing a coat?" I demanded, sounding like my mom. "It is colder than..." numerous colorful comparisons came to mind, but I didn't say them out loud.

"Couldn't find it." She muttered.

I removed my own jacket, unzipped the fleece lining and handed it over to her. She hesitated then took it from me and put it on.

After a moment she whispered, "I'm not entirely sure yet what it is, Sean. I just know that something isn't right."

"I assumed you don't mean losing your coat." I pulled the outer layer of my ski parka back on. "You'll have to do better than that if you want me to understand what you are talking about."

She let out a deep sigh and closed her notebook. "Look, all I know is that, if you count Cherie's picture, all of the projects we did in art class are accounted for. But there was an extra one, the other one that was missing. Who did that picture?"

I shrugged, "What does it matter? It is just a picture of Santa's reindeer, or whatever."

"Precisely!" Bronnie pointed at my chest. "What does it matter? Who would make, or take a kid's picture off the wall at a school? And who would do it so carelessly that they accidentally took the picture next to it and tore it off the wall?"

"Ah, so you think that is what happened? The pages got taped together or something and when they took the mystery picture, they took Cherie's too?"

"Yup." She nodded.

"Maybe someone made two, or maybe it was a picture from a different class and the art teacher took it down?" I was thinking out loud. "Maybe it just got caught on someone as they walk by."

Bronnie shook her head. "If a teacher removed it, they would not have been so careless. And I would not expect anyone just to throw it in the rubbish bin. This person was in a hurry. They kept the one project and not the other."

I contemplated her logic, "Which makes me wonder," I said, "how did you know which way down the hall they went?"

She looked at me in eagerly. "The way the little scrap of paper was still stuck to the wall. It had been pulled off the wall from the right side, most likely as they walked down the hall accidentally taking Cherie's with it. If they had taken more carefully or from the other side, her project might have been torn, but still would have been hanging there, of course."

"Of course," I said, trying to imagine the mystery person, grabbing the mystery picture, in that crowded hallway. "How do you know they didn't catch on it by accident or something? There were a ton of people that night."

"Both pieces of art would have been in the trash." She opened her notebook again. "No, it is too strange. Next time there is an extra picture on the wall, I will get the name on it."

"So you are telling me that not only is there a renegade artist in the school posting all over the place, but we also have a renegade art thief?" I looked over both shoulders. "Quick, someone alert the media!"

"Ha, ha, Sean. This is serious."

"Is it?" I asked.

She exhaled. "Maybe. I don't know. But if you see art work with a name you don't recognize, tell me."

I saluted.

As it turned out, looking at pictures on the wall again was unnecessary.

Our music teacher had been hard at work preparing a holiday concert event to dwarf all others. Bronnie not only played the violin, she was tremendous at it. And so she was scheduled to accompany to some of the carols we sang and then perform solo.

The two classes from our grade were gathered in the music room before our performance. Mrs. Andrews was festive in a red velvet jacket and white fur cuffs as she double-checked our more drab matching white shirts and black pants. When she had finished inspection, Bronnie tugged me into the corner of the room. She looked around and then shoved a folded piece of paper into my hand.

"Look at that." She said.

I glanced down at the paper and lifted my eyebrows. It was only the program from the night's performance. There were blue snowflakes printed on the paper, the playlist of songs and the names of the students performing.

It didn't take me long to realize what she was showing me. Slowly, I counted the number of students on the paper. Even those who didn't show up for the concert would still be printed, the whole grade. "There are 93 kids on this list."

A smile formed on her lips. "Well played, Mr. Watkins."

"Do you know who the add-on is?" I asked her.

Bronnie smiled again, this time more like a sly fox. "Bethany Grieves."

"Who the heck is that?" I asked.

Bronnie jabbed the program with her finger. "Exactly."

The fourth grade's rendition of "Diwali Dance" was the upper school's cue to move out of the music room. Our grade formed a line around the back of the auditorium, onto the stage and, one by one ascended onto risers looking out over the family and friends of the entire school. Bronnie was the last onto the stage, cradling her violin. She took her place stage right. Even though she could probably play the upcoming songs in her sleep, she seemed agitated and nervous.

Every moment there was a break in the instrumental, her eyes would scan the crowd. She scrutinized the audience, then the class on stage, then the audience again. I didn't know what she was searching for, but she was distracted enough for me to lose focus. I had to completely ignore her to remember the words to the songs. It seemed impossible that she could play so well when her mind was clearly engaged elsewhere, but she made it through with fewer mistakes than I did.

The concert ended and as we bowed. Bronnie dipped her head, her massive curls flopped down. She used her free hand to lift her hair from her face and as she did, her eyes opened wide and fixed on something in the rear of the room. I followed her gaze and watched as a short, dark haired man in gray suit ducked out of the cafeteria door and was gone.

After the performance, when families and kids were finding each other, she grabbed me by the arm. "Did you see him?"

"Ow!" I grunted and removed her hand. "Yeah, the guy in the back? He left the concert early."

Bronnie nodded. "Precisely. He left quickly and alone, as far as I could tell. No kids."

That was the last we got to discuss the events of the concert. Our parents converged on us from different directions and it was the first time I got to see Bronnie's father. His broad frame towered over the other adults as well as the kids. For the first time I saw where Bronnie got her fashion sense. Mr. Browne was in a tailored suit that he wore with ease, combined with his salt and pepper hair and mahogany skin, I thought he looked more like a famous actor than a suburban dad.

Bronnie leaned over and whispered to me, "Sorry if my dad seems nervous. He isn't so great at meeting new people."

"He's nervous?" I jibed. If Mr. Browne was anxious, he hid it well. I think we kids wore identical embarrassed expressions as our parents were introduced, then proceeded to trade anecdotes about us and and make plans for a double-date night after holiday vacations.

Yeah, what could go wrong with that?

Chapter 6

The gloomy and rainy winter days had
finally given over to snow sparkling in
the bright sunshine, even if we had to
drive two hundred miles to accomplish
that feat.

My bedroom curtains were
purposefully drawn tightly shut against
the morning glare. I was sore and
exhausted from the awkward first days
on the slopes and was doing my best to
sleep it off. Still, the combination of a
pulsating light and an obnoxious bird
song made me pull my pillow tightly
over my head. I tried to ignore them

both, but it was no use. The bird would take a rest for a few moments, then restart it's relentless tweeting.

Reluctantly my brain came to the realization that I needed to wake up. Checking the time on my bedside table, I saw that the light and the tweeting were both coming from my tablet. Someone was trying to call me. Burying my head in the pillow one last time, I relented and picked up the screen to find that Bronnie was trying to engage in a video chat.

I was too tired to really come up with an evasive plan and simply accepted the call so my tablet would stop making that infernal noise.

"What?" I said, groggy and hoarse.

Bronnie was entirely too chipper, "And a very good morning to you, sleepy head. Aching from yesterday?"

There comes the point in time when you stop questioning strange things in your life and just go with the flow. This moment was apparently it for me. I didn't much care how she knew I was sore. And she was smart enough to know I would be asleep in bed and yet she called anyway.

I answered, "Yes, I'm very uncomfortable, thank you for asking. I fell on the first descent yesterday, taking out my dad, a temporary fence, and almost a hot cocoa stand. Not my finest moment. How have you been?"

Bronnie snickered. "Excellent, thank you. So I wanted to ask you a question."

"I figured that."

"Could there be a reason, a medical reason I mean, that someone would be listed on our classroom student list, and do art projects, but never actually be in the building itself?"

I rubbed my face with my hand and pushed myself to a sitting position. "Probably. Mono is fairly common illness among kids." According to the small camera window on my screen, I was sporting some epic bedhead.

Bronnie tilted her head back and set her chin on her thumb in thought.

I clarified. "Mononucleosis. It's a virus and is contagious. Makes the patient extremely tired so they usually can't handle the rigors of being at school." Bronnie nodded so I continued, "Lyme disease, I'm learning is also common in our area, and causes some kids to stay home for long time."

"Hmmm..." Bronnie contemplated. "Social media didn't show anyone named Bethany in our area with cancers or extreme hereditary disorders. None for which people create awareness or fundraiser campaigns, anyway, so I was curious..." I heard someone speaking to her in the background, but she raised her hand, signaling them to give her a moment. "Is there a chance this Bethany could be homeschooled?"

"Possibly. She also could be, like, six inches tall and we just didn't notice her."

"If she were six inches tall her artwork would be miniscule."

I laughed, then inspected the mass produced artwork on the walls of our rented condo. "You know, most times homeschooled kids won't show up on a class roster. At least in West Virginia they didn't. I knew of at least five homeschooled students when I lived there and they certainly didn't have any art on the walls. Their parents reported directly to the board of education, not the individual schools."

"Still," Bronnie mused, "it is worth checking, to see if our district does things differently. And I would have noticed a six-inch tall kid in our class."

I sighed. "Of course you would have. OK, I will ask dad if he knows any kids who are homeschooling because of illness. Even if Bethany isn't his patient, he might know of a contagion going around. It's a small town, after all."

"Thanks," Bronnie said, "and I will check with homeschool parent groups for this Bethany."

"OK," and then a thought occurred to me, "Why do you care about this so much, anyway?"

"I don't know. Something just doesn't feel right and I want," she thought for a moment, "I need to get to the bottom of it."

"I understand." I nodded. "Now why don't you enjoy the break and go do something...I dunno...British."

"You mean drink tea?" She said, with a smile.

"Yeah. And watch soccer."

"You mean football."

"Whatever."

"Ok, you go do something American. Like eat cereal and bacon."

"I plan to. Text me if you find out anything and I'll do the same."

She clicked off and I put the tablet back on the bedside table. Then I face planted directly onto my pillow. It was no use though. My stomach wanted food, my heart wanted anime cartoons and my brain wanted answers. Darn that girl.

I shuffled towards the living room of our rental condo, which had three bedrooms down a short hallway, leading to an open kitchen and living area with a balcony. It was decorated in an early 1990s catalog style with plaid recliners and cheap landscape paintings.

The room was blissfully silent and calm, which was a sure sign of the toddler still asleep. Margot was sharing a room with my brother who, although fifteen years older than she was, had remarkably similar sleep patterns. They stayed up late, slept late and had beds which resembled nests of wild animals when they woke.

My parents were soaking up the morning peace and quiet as well. Still wearing flannel pajamas, they gazed out of the picture window at the snow while drinking coffee. I followed their gaze to see some skiers who were already hitting the slopes.

My mom turned around. "Good morning, Sean. We didn't expect you up so soon."

"Morning," I said and shuffled my new moose antler slippers into the kitchen for cereal and a big glass of chocolate milk. "I would still be asleep, except for Bronnie calling me from England."

I saw dad give mom a wink.

"We thought we heard you talking." Mom said, ever the diplomat." What did she want?"

"Not much." Trying to sound nonchalant to keep any teasing at bay.

I finished pouring the milk and sat down at the table before fully answering. "Remember how I told you she enjoys solving mysteries?"

Dad responded, "Oh yes, quite the detective friend you have."

"Yeah. Well, she has discovered that there is a ghost student in our school."

That got their attention.

"A ghost student?" Dad repeated.

Perfect set up to ask him about any students having mono. "Well, not really a ghost as in, like, the disembodied soul of a dead person. More like a student we can't find. She has noticed that there is artwork on the walls at school that doesn't belong to anyone in our class. Also, there was a kid listed on our winter concert program who is definitely not in our class. Stuff like that." I took a drink of milk and let that sink in.

"My, Bronnie is very observant, isn't she." My mom mused and peered out of the window again over the top of her mug.

I nodded and responded, "That isn't the half of it. She wanted me to know if there might be medical reason why someone's work or name would be popping up around the school, but student not actually attend class?"

My dad contemplated this question for a moment and scratched at the gray chin scruff he had yet to shave off. His bedhead was almost as bad as mine. "I suppose you already thought of mono."

"Yeah." I said and mentally patted myself on the back. "Anyone you know with mono?"

Dad took a drink of his coffee too, "You know I'm not allowed to discuss specific patients, but in general, no. I've not treated anyone in your grade. There was a county bulletin circulated in October about a high schooler with mononucleosis, but the student is question is not in your district."

Mom laughed, "You sound entirely too official for a leisurely vacation morning."

"You're right, I do." He got up to bring the coffee pot back to the table. The brew was so thick and dark it looked more like molasses, with foam on top. They never used filters and never,

ever a coffee machine. Dad said they developed the taste for this coffee when they were stationed in Turkey, but that is the most they ever mentioned living there.

Mom chewed on her thumbnail, which was her habit when she was thinking. "I suppose your ghost student could be home schooled. I would imagine if they have art work and such up on the walls, maybe they did attended your school at one time or another."

That theory, of Bethany having gone to Captain's Watch earlier, wasn't one I considered when it came to home schooling. After I finished breakfast, I sent Bronnie a quick text message before getting dressed. It was promising to be another great day on the slopes

and I didn't want to miss a single
second of it. I had my snow pants half
on when my phone whistled in response.

BB-Bronnie

*Dad says no students of our age in our
town with mono. Says doctors get
notified in case of outbreaks.*

*Negative here on home schooled parent
groups with a child named Bethany.
How did you find out so fast?*

*Hacked the group forums. Not patient
enough to wait for them to approve me
into their groups.*

*I'll pretend I didn't read that. Off to
tumble down the mountain again.*

*Let me know if you find out anything
else.*

Also Don't get arrested

She gave me a thumbs up. I ended our chat with a happy face and a snowflake, then made my way out to the kitchen again for a last minute snack.

BB-Bronnie

This research is entirely too frustrating via computer. Some things I will finish when we get back. Some records only in hard copy.

OK, enjoy ur vacation and don't spend the whole time working

She was probably already asleep, with London being about 5 hours ahead of us, but I sent it anyway.

Then Bronnie herself ghosted, not contacting me at all the rest of the break. She was practically jumping out of her seat when I stepped on the bus the first day back at school. She motioned for me to sit next to her. Her blue down parka had been replaced by a bright crimson hooded cape. All she needed was a basket full of goodies to take grandma's house. I barely managed to say "what's up?" before she grabbed my arm.

"I found her!" Bronnie whispered to me but her voice conveyed it with so much enthusiasm I looked around to see if anyone else had heard.

"You found who?" I said automatically, before really registering what she had told me.

She was exasperated with my response. "Bethany Grieves! I found her!" She whisper-shouted, if there is such a thing.

"How?" I whispered back.

"Well, I found out who she is, anyway, not where she is. I did a search of public records online." She opened her backpack and took out some loose papers. "These are print outs from the county database."

"Do I want to know how you got these?" I reluctantly took the papers and surveyed the lines she had marked with a purple highlighter.

Bronnie recited from memory the text that I was reading. "Bethany Grieves, born May 12, 2004, to Elizabeth Raines Grieves and Emmanuel Grieves." She had been born in the local county hospital.

"Turn the page." She said.

There was a marriage record for Elizabeth and Emmanuel from the year before, and a divorce record from 2010. There was no mention of Bethany in the divorce records, however.

I gave the papers back and shrugged my shoulders, "What is the big deal?"

She retrieved another stack of printouts with Bethany's name referenced in soccer tournaments, elementary school art shows and even a recent Facebook page for Elizabeth Raines, appearing to have dropped the Grieves surname after her divorce.

Bronnie bobbed her head to an inaudible beat. "She is real. She exists Sean, or did exist. Now all we have to do is find her."

"What do you mean 'we have to find her'?" I peered at my friend. Her gaze was locked on mine, he eyes widened at my response. I wondered exactly what kind of pinball game thought processes were going on inside that head of hers. "You are never going to let this go, are you?" I relented.

She beamed in triumph. "Not a chance."

I sighed the exact same way my parents do when my little sister wants something and they know resistance is futile.

"Ok then. What is our next move?"

Bronnie clapped her hands. "Is it possible your mum will take us to the main branch of the county library this week?" She asked. "Not this evening, I have Krav Maga, but perhaps tomorrow directly after school. My mum is on committee almost every evening until March."

"Probably. What are we looking for? More public records or birth certificates?"

"Better than that," she grinned, "Yearbooks."

Wow, yearbooks, with complete strangers in them. Joy of joys.

Interlude:

It used to be you had to make your own "go bag". Now, you can buy them premade. Backpacks full of everything you might need in an emergency. Usually they are stocked with stuff for people leaving natural disasters or those afraid of war and zombie apocalypses. Ready made meals, medicine, water purification tablets and all that jazz.

I kept one along with a suitcase of spare clothes and one of Bethany's favorite toys in the trunk of our second car. If my ex did ever show up, I could ditch our old lives in exactly 2 minutes. All I had to do was get Bethany and get to our second car, which was parked in the lot of a local nursing home. While working there briefly I learned that many residents who no longer drove, still held an attachment to their old automobiles. Behind the main residence building sat a row of almost abandoned, barely used cars.

So that day, while my ex was writhing on the ground in bear-mace induced agony, I picked up my daughter from the sitter and ditched our old car at a bus stop. We rode the bus to the nursing home, got in the old Buick I had hidden amongst the retirees vehicles and left town for good. Again.

Bethany said nothing, but I could tell we both hoped it would be the last time we would need our go bags. The last time we would need to build new lives.

I'd have to be smarter.

Chapter 7

If the weather had been better, I would have considered ditching the library for the skate park again. Mother nature, it seemed, was determined to have me go. She sent down the bleakest combination of sleet, fog and general loathing I had seen in years. She was still withholding the snow from coastal dwellers and so we were resigned to what felt more like freezer burn than a winter wonderland.

My mom picked us up from school and drove us to the center of the county, which in addition to being the location of the closest Target was also that of the central library. I sat in the rear of our German station wagon and watched my little sister shoot dry cereal all over the place like a curly haired Gatling gun. Bronnie had taken the front passenger seat, but only after I conceded to my mom that it was polite to let a guest sit up front and, also, as a newly immigrated Brit she couldn't possibly be expected to know how "calling shotgun" meant.

"Bronnie, honey," my mom asked, "what is it you need to find at the main library? Usually, Sean does most of his research on the computer or we request books to be sent over to our branch. Not that I mind taking you at all."

Bronnie shifted in her seat to face more towards my mother. "I'm looking to learn more about the colonies for our history class and I thought the larger library might have a better selection of materials. I found a list of reference materials on the Internet, but reading them online isn't ideal. I'm rather old-fashioned in that way." She lied.

"I do appreciate you taking us, Mrs. Watkins. I hope it doesn't interfere with your day." She quickly added.

My mom was chipper, "Not at all. Margot and I have a few errands to run in town, this gives me a good excuse to get out of the office."

"So I take it your work is not a standard office job?" Bronnie asked casually. She was probing my mom and I knew it. I wanted to nudge her, but my sister's gigantic, astronaut style car seat was in the way.

My mother didn't seem phased by the inquiry. "I'm a consultant. So you are correct, the hours vary from day to day. Right now, after the holidays, it is a little slow."

Bronnie probed further. "Your move to West Virginia, was it for your work or your husband's?"

"For his schooling. There is an excellent school of osteopathic medicine there." Mom said before aiming some mumbled expletives and instructions about the proper use of a blinker at the truck in front of us.

"And then you moved here? Instead of going back to California?"

My mom glanced at Bronnie, then at me in the rearview mirror. She evaded the question. "California was getting too expensive for us."

Bronnie fluttered her eyebrows and nodded.

My mom dropped us at the front of the library. "Call me when you are finished and I will do the same." She smiled. "Whoever is done first gets to pick dinner!"

"Right, let's get to it!" I said, already planning to suggest Vietnamese noodle soup in order to combat the terrible cold weather.

Bronnie made a direct line for the front door, which I caught just as it was closing behind her. "Why did we need to come here in the first place? Why not just our local library?"

"I already went there and looked at the yearbooks for Bethany Grieves, she wasn't in any of them. Obviously our current school yearbook hasn't yet been published."

The library was a cavernous and modern building, as large as any warehouse store. It was two levels, built in the shape of a U. The upstairs was almost entirely open to the floor below. It held a few rows of books, but was mostly work desks, comfortable reading chairs and meeting rooms. On the main level, bookcase after bookcase radiated out from the center staircase like spokes of a wheel. The majority of the ceiling was glass, showing a gray and cloudy twilight sky

Bronnie made her way to the information desk, nearest the stairs. A grandfatherly old man, with half-rimmed reading glasses, unruly eyebrows and a green bow tie smiled at us as we approached the information counter.

"Excuse me, but could you please tell us where the yearbooks are for the local county schools?" I asked as Bronnie took in our surroundings.

"Well, that is a question you don't hear every day." He replied with a grin.

Bronnie innocently twirled her curly hair, "We are doing a project for history class."

"Ah," he smiled, "local families and all that?" He nodded came around from behind the desk, "Follow me."

He was quick for an older man, scooting adeptly past rows of gardening books, romance novels, and movies on DVD. Finally, tucked in the far right corner of the building, near the fire escape, was a collection of local periodicals. Magazines lined the walls, displayed on angled shelves to showcase their fronts rather than the spines. The smell of newspaper ink and dust gave it a much different vibe than the vibrant children's and young adult sections I was used to perusing.

The man gestured to the row of yearbooks, all neatly organized by school and year. He then wished us luck and disappeared around the corner. I was overwhelmed for a moment by the sheer number of volumes facing us, but Bronnie was undeterred. She found the sections for local elementary schools and pulled off every book for the past seven years, stacking them in my arms without even turning her head.

When at last we had retrieved the last of the records for all fifteen elementary schools in the county, we trudged to an open table set them down with a loud thunk.

At first, we began at the front of each book, turning the pages one by one, but I quickly got impatient. Instead, I flipped to the back pages of the yearbooks where most held a glossary of names. After searching two yearbooks for Everley Elementary, I practically jumped out of my chair, "I found her!"

Bronnie looked up, "You did? That was fast." She said, coming to look over my shoulder. I took some satisfaction in finding Bethany first, but only a tiny bit. We turned to the page indicated by the glossary. My heart skipped a beat. There on the page, was our ghost student.

Second-grader Bethany Grieves smiled sweetly at us from the page. She had light brown curly hair, just long enough to touch her shoulders. Her baby cheeks were still evident and she was missing a front tooth. She wore a pink striped shirt and her hands were folded neatly in her lap.

I tapped my finger on the page. "That is her. Wow." We both stared at her for a beat or two. "She kind of looks like you." I finally commented.

Bronnie tilted her head as she studied the photo. "Somewhat."

Bethany's ringlets were not as dark as Bronnie's, nor as tightly wound. Her skin was more pinkish brown and she had lighter eyes, maybe blue, from what I could tell. Obviously she was a lot younger in this photo, but the similarities were still there.

"What do we do next?" I asked.

"We keep searching until we find her for all of the other years up to middle school." Bronnie pointed to the stack of other Everly yearbooks. "Give me one, I'll help go through them"

I shook my head, "No need, she isn't in them."

"What do you mean?" she asked, "How could you have gone through them so quickly?"

I shrugged, "I just looked in the glossaries, it is a lot faster."

She smacked her forehead with her palm. "Gah." She eyed the other stacks. "I suppose for now that will work. We will need to really comb through the yearbooks where she is listed, however, to make sure we don't miss anything."

We moved on to other schools and found her elsewhere quickly. Kindergarten at Cliffside Elementary, first grade at Green Valley, third at Janney, and fourth at Culper's Run.

"How do you know to look for the years up to middle school?" I wondered.

"First, based on the fact that her artwork and other things are being placed in our middle school." She flipped a book closed and opened another. "Secondly, that second-grade yearbook you found is from five years ago."

"Right on," I said.

"Found her again!" Bronnie chimed.

We went on until we had found all seven yearbooks then laid them chronologically next to one another, all open to Bethany's page. Her sweet smile stared back at us, from Kindergarten to sixth grade. Each year she appeared a touch older, her hair a little longer, her chubby cheeks slimming down. She was getting dimples. Each year she wore a different shirt, but had the same upright pose. The same curls held back by a clip or a headband.

I studied the books. "She sure moves around a lot."

Bronnie nodded slowly. "Seven years, seven schools, seven towns, three different counties. Does anything seem off to you?"

"The whole thing seems totally off to me," I said, stacking up the failed yearbooks and shelving them in order to ignore the goose bumps that had appeared on my arms.

"Look at her." She pointed to the pages. "I mean really look at her."

We posed identically, arms crossed and gazes fierce. We must have stood there like statues, looking at the yearbooks, for at least two minutes, which felt much longer.

Finally, glancing back at the second grade photo, I spoke. "I give up, I don't see it. She is a cute little kid, nice smile."

"That's it!" Bronnie finally exclaimed, and slapped me on the shoulder and pointed back at the table. "It *is* a nice smile! They are all nice smiles."

My forehead wrinkled instinctively. "Huh?"

"She has the same smile, Sean, the exact same smile in every picture. It doesn't change, she doesn't change."

"Sure she does," I said, putting the last useless book on the shelf and returning. "Look, she gets older, her hair gets longer."

"But Bethany doesn't change, not really. She has the same pose, the same smile, the same hands in her lap. Even her blouse, the pattern and the color on it changes, but the style doesn't."

I inspected the pictures more carefully and Bronnie was right. The little girl seemed to age in the picture, but the major characteristics of those photos were identical. "It looks like an age progression program was run, or someone Photoshopped it manually."

"Such as when the police surmise what a person might look like 10 years from their last picture." Bronnie tapped her nails on the table. "Why would someone edit age progression pictures of a kid and then stick them into all of these yearbooks."

I shrugged and was about to answer when we were startled by a voice behind us. We both turned around as we jumped.

"Did you find what you were looking for?" The man from the information desk asked as he came closer. Bronnie stealthily closed the yearbooks behind her back.

"Oh yes, so far." She answered. "May we take these home?"

He shook his head and wiped his glasses with a small cloth, "No, sorry. These are the only copies we have, so they have to remain in the building. You are welcome to make copies of any pages you need." He gestured to a photocopier against the opposite wall.

"Thank you." I said.

"Let me know if you need anything else. We have change at the desk." With that, he left again.

I turned to Bronnie, "The sign on the copier says ten cents each. Do you have any money with you?"

"Yes, I have a some." She handed me a change purse from her backpack and said, "Make photocopies, would you? I will see if she appears elsewhere in the books."

She opened the top yearbook and ran her finger down the list of names in the glossary while I dug through the change purse, fishing out little dimes.

My phone rang. "Hi mom," I said, holding the phone to my ear with my shoulder, instantly bummed she had finished her errands before we were done and would therefore be choosing dinner.

"Hey, sweetie. How's it going?" she replied, I could hear voices in the background.

I dumped a few coins on the table. "Good, almost done. We are just about to make some copies." Just then I heard Bronnie draw in a huge breath. I mouthed the word "what?" to her. She glared at me, wide-eyed and gestured with her hands to come over to her.

My mom kept talking, "Well, I finished at the store early. Margot lost her mind in the Hot Wheels aisle. Do you need more time or should I come get you now." Bronnie evidently heard this because she waved her hands and mouthed "Not yet".

"We need a few more minutes."

The phone was silent for a moment, I could hear rustling. "Ok, hun. I'll pack the car and then go grab some takeout for dinner. Couple more minutes."

"Ok, thanks," and then I added "Pho please!" as an afterthought. It was worth a try.

I slid the phone back into my pocket and sat down next to Bronnie. She had three of the yearbooks opened to the glossary pages again. Bronnie was opening the fourth book but gestured to the ones already on the table. "Tell me what you see, Sean."

I gazed down at the yearbooks. The pages were all open to the listing that had Bethany's name on it. "I see names," I said, "lots of names, Bethany Grieves included."

She put the fourth next to the others and opened the last yearbook. "Look carefully, go down the list until you get to Bethany's name."

On some pages, her name was closer to the top than others. I whispered the names on the pages to myself; they were alphabetized by last names. D, E, F, G for Grieves. By the third book, I saw what Bronnie had seen. "Faraday.

Jennifer Faraday. She is on all three of these lists."

Bronnie placed the Culper's Run yearbook on the table, "She is in all five of these." She pointed to the two I had at the copier. "I bet you Jennifer Faraday is in those two as well."

We both made note of the pages that Jennifer Faraday was on and turned to them. I drew in a breath, "That's her alright. Miss Faraday, our school secretary!"

Bronnie was humming, "In this one, she is listed as a teacher's assistant for third grade."

"Attendance secretary at Green Valley." I replied.

"Parental liaison, whatever that is, at Janney." Bronnie went to the copier.

"Long term substitute position at Cliffside."

"What on earth would Miss Faraday have to do with Bethany Grieves?" I thought out loud.

Bronnie shook her head, "This cannot be a coincidence."

We copied all of the glossary pages, just to be sure, and made additional copies of the pictures of both Bethany and Miss Faraday. We ran out of dimes half of the way through, but a blue-haired teenager, who passed by to get a woodworking magazine, made change for a few quarters.

The nice man at the desk was there still when we made our way to the door.

"Successful trip I trust?" He said.

Bronnie nodded emphatically. "Yes, we appreciate your help."

He slapped the desk gently. "Oh, I'm glad. Not many people come to look at those old things, especially not kids like you."

"Yeah," I said in an off-handed way, "Not much use for old yearbooks I guess."

He put his glasses back on. "Oh, we do get a few people looking for them. Some older folks getting nostalgic or looking for lost friends. We have one research regular.

"Really?" Bronnie stopped and turned back to the desk. Her interest was piqued. "What kind of research?"

"He *says* it is genealogy. He is working on the history of the county and the original families who formed it." He stacked some papers. "Always makes me wonder about him, though."

"Wonder what?" I asked.

The man shrugged. "I might be talking out of turn, but he just gives me the willies. He says he does genealogy research but never looks in anything but the newer yearbooks. Couple of times I tried to show him the records room with the historic marriage records and land grants, but he isn't interested. It makes a person wonder." He sighed. "Then again, maybe I'm only bored and reading too much into it. That can happen in a library. Reading too much into it." He winked and chuckled at his own joke.

I heard a car horn beep and saw my mom's station wagon through the window. "We have to go. Thank you very much for your help."

"My pleasure." He returned and I heard him say to the next lady at the counter as we left, "Such polite young kids, those two."

We ran from the vestibule to the car, shielding our papers from the sleet. My stomach grumbled. I was looking forward to the take out mom had gotten, which from the smell was soup like I had hoped. Bronnie interrupted my thoughts of my stomach, "Are you thinking what I'm thinking?" she asked.

"Probably not, unless you are thinking about Vietnamese noodle soup," I answered though she didn't seem to get the joke.

The next morning dawned warm and sunny like a new spring day..

Just kidding, it was rainy and cold and sucky. Again.

I was anxious to hear what kind of conclusion Bronnie had formed about the printouts and yearbooks, because surely she had been up all night contemplating them. She wasn't on the bus though, and she wasn't in class either. I was so distracted thinking about her and our recent discovery, that by lunch Mrs. Andrews even asked if I was feeling well enough to continue the day.

When school finally let out and I got home, I saw there were numerous text messages and emails from Bronnie waiting for me on my phone. They went like this:

BB-Bronnie

Where are you?
Oh yeah, you are in school. Call me when you get out of school.
Are you out yet?
You better not be ignoring me. Or at the skate park.
It is 3:05, where are you?

A fleeting thought of what it might be like having Bronnie as a wife passed through my mind, giving me a shudder. I picked up the phone to call her back, but the phone rang in my hand before I could hit send.

"Hi Bronnie."

She was out of breath. "Where have you been?"

I poured myself a glass of juice and rolled my eyes. "A better question is where have you been? Since you clearly weren't in school."

Bronnie was apparently eating something crunchy, probably chips. "I took a personal day, too many things to do."

"Kids don't get personal days. What did you do on your day off? Go to the spa?"

"Puh," Bronnie puffed, "I've been hacking."

Oh, God. I put my hand on my head. This must be what it feels like to be a parent. "Hacking into what, exactly?"

She must have caught my tone because she corrected herself, "To be precise, more researching and digging than actual hacking. Most court and arrest records are public domain. There might have been a guessed password or two and a backdoor server entry, basic SQL queries, nothing terribly dodgy."

Would the police use metal handcuffs or those plastic zip tie things on us when they took us to juvie? Criminal records add some pizzazz to college applications, right? "Christ, Bronnie, you can't just go around hacking into government computers."

"Can't?" She retorted.

"Shouldn't."

I heard her drinking the last of a beverage noisily through a straw.

"Regardless, I need you to come over. I need a sounding board."

"Now?"

"Now."

"Ugh, fine." That's me Sean Watkins, human sounding board. At your service.

I hung up without another word and looked out of the window. The rain had let up, but it was still windy and probably barely above the freezing mark. I knocked on the door of my mom's home office. She was on the phone, but waived me in and smiled. Where Bronnie had two monitors on her desk, my mom had three. One computer screen showed a bunch of unread emails, another a spreadsheet of numbers, a third was a satellite image of somewhere barren, it looked like a paint swatch for multiple shades of beige. She clicked the power off on that last screen, then rolled her eyes at her phone and made a talking gesture with her hand.

Sometimes she got stuck on calls like this. So I used one of her sticky notes to write her a message and handed it over.

It read, "Bronnie was absent today. I am going to take her our homework assignments for tonight. Not contagious." The last bit as a preemptive strike.

Mom nodded and kissed me on my cheek before I left. I grabbed my backpack and my board.

Mr. Jenkins and I sped along the road, splashing in puddles and daring the slick pavement. Despite the exertion, the chilly, wet air did its damage. My teeth were chattering when I arrived. Bronnie must have been ready for me because I sailed directly into her open garage as instructed instead of hopping up to the porch. The surveillance mirror inside the garage had been joined by a small camera.

I opened the door to the house, which led through an enormous and very organized mudroom, to a workshop and then to the back stairs leading to her room. Bronnie was at the kitchen table, however, typing away furiously on her laptop.

"What took you so long?" She said.

"Good to see you too." I returned. "What's with the camera?"

She looked up from the computer. "I decided the system needed an upgrade."

Bronnie was wearing men's style black cotton pajamas and furry dog slippers with floppy ears. The table was littered with printed photos. Various student and school photos with the same curly haired girl somewhere in them, usually out of focus, but now circled in marker.

Others photos were of a dark haired man. One of them I recognized as being taken at the corner of the Browne's picket fence, near the sidewalk.

She stacked the pictures together and peered up at me. "Do you want the good news, the bizarre news or the bad news?"

"Chronological order, I suppose." I answered while gesturing to a plate of scones on the table. Bronnie nodded for me to take one and pushed a cup of hot tea my way. I suppose in England even kids drink tea. It wasn't bad to follow the scone with.

I sat down across the table from her with my snack. "So hit me."

Bronnie leaned back and crossed her arms. "For starters, Bethany Grieves is real, or was real, as far as I can tell." Bronnie pushed her laptop to me then helped herself to a scone and picked at it absently.

I found myself looking at a the electronic file of birth records for our county from over ten years ago, the same one Bronnie has showed me on the bus.

Bethany Anne Grieves, born December 4, 2003 at the county hospital at 4:23 am to parents Elizabeth Raines Grieves and Emmanuel Grieves (no middle).

"Huh." I said. "So is that the good news?"

She clicked on the laptop and opened another window for me to look at.

Probably illegally downloaded documents with official headers were arranged across her desktop. "What am I looking at here?"

She pointed to the one page. "Public court documents for a divorce between Elizabeth and Emmanuel Grieves." She pointed to their names at the top. Elizabeth by the title "Plaintiff" and the Emmanuel by the name "Defendant".

I sighed. "Do I even want to know where you got this?"

"Probably not."

"Is that the weird thing? Because people get divorced all of the time."

Bronnie pointed to the date. "Look at when they got divorced. It would have been the year Bethany entered kindergarten."

"Ooookaaaaaaaaaay." I really didn't see where this was going.

"And, you see what it says there? It says the divorce was uncontested. Which means that either Emmanuel didn't complain or didn't show up for court."

She pulled up another paper, another court document. This one was from earlier in the year, "Hey, I told you chronological order."

She shrugged, "More drama this way."

I exclaimed. "This is an arrest warrant!"

Bronnie nodded slowly and smugly, her arms crossed in triumph. "A warrant for Emmanuel Grieves arrest, for assault and battery, as well as abuse of a minor."

I pushed the computer away and drank some tea to help get rid of the chills and goose bumps I was feeling.

I glanced at Bronnie, her eyes were focused and intense. "So our ghost student, Bethany, was born for real. Had parents for real, then dad went to jail and parents got a divorced, for real. Is that right?"

"Almost." Bronnie leaned forward. "Nothing happened after the original warrant. I can't find records of a trial, sentencing or incarceration records. The divorce was granted and Elizabeth Raines got full custody of Bethany. Maybe I missed something, maybe he was arrested somewhere else and is serving time totally unrelated to this. I don't know the full story of what happened after, but I think we know who does."

"Who?" I asked, but Bronnie didn't answer. She merely grinned at me.

I held up my hands. "Wait, no. Not Mrs. Farraday?"

Bronnie clapped her hands.

"Oh my god, Bronnie, you can't just ask her!"

"Why not?"

"What do you mean why not? What, you are just going to walk into school tomorrow and be all 'Good morning Miss Farraday. Is it pizza again for lunch? Good. By the way, how do you know Bethany Grieves.'" I said. "She is an adult, an employee at the school. You could get in serious trouble."

"Possibly," Bronnie smirked.

There was a feeling in the pit of my stomach, which made me believe I might not have to play sick tomorrow. Which wouldn't really be like lying. If she went through with the plan, I would probably hurl for real.

Chapter 8

That night over pot roast and mashed potatoes, I got up the courage to ask my parents a question that had been bugging me.

"Mom, Dad, what does 'assault and battery' mean?" I asked.

Dad choked on his steak and mom dropped her fork.

"I swear I didn't touch him!" My older brother blurted out, a look of innocence on his face.

"God, not you, Duke." I retorted. My older brother was named for surfing legend Duke Kahanamoku, but he did not inherit any kind of the legend's coolness. I like to think I received the Hawaiian charisma, if not the name.

Probably I was dreaming.

Mom took a gulp of wine. "Where did you hear about assault and battery?"

I was prepared for this question. "Oh, I read it in a news article. The police said that a suspect was wanted for assault and battery." Boom. Reading is always a great excuse, parents love it when you read, especially current events.

Dad stared straight ahead as if to say *you take this one*. Mom caught his gaze and took a deep breath.

She said, "Legally it is to threaten someone and then harm or attempt to harm them."

"Oh," I said, "You mean like to beat someone up?"

"Sometimes." Mom refilled her glass, more than usual. "The severity of injury isn't so much the focus of the charge. Simply attempting to do harm is illegal, touching someone without their permission is illegal, even if you don't hurt them. But all of that said, assault and battery is a serious crime and the police don't toss those terms around lightly."

I nodded and chewed. This Emmanuel Grieves wasn't sounding like anyone I wanted to meet. Ever. And the fact that Bronnie seemed to be actively chasing after him made me feel even worse.

Sleep didn't come easily that night. Even though I had never really seen him, and had no idea what he looked like, Emmanuel Grieves was in my thoughts anyway. In my head, he looked like a combination of Blackbeard the Pirate crossed with a 1990's horror movie bad guy. Slick hair, bad teeth and a skinny tie. He would pop up from around corners in hallways, under cabinets in the kitchen, and (the one that jolted me from my sleep) out from the trunk of my dad's van.

Needless to say, I was not in prime form when I saw Bronnie that next morning on the bus. She didn't appear to be in great shape either. She thanked me for bringing her the homework and asked if I had any thoughts on our upcoming class projects. Beyond that, she kept to herself.

Maybe she had finally given up on this whole non-existent student thing. We could go back to being regular kids without fear of finding out what the inside of a jail cell looks like. Or maybe without incurring the wrath of someone who runs from assault charges. Perhaps I could get a regular night's sleep again, with normal nightmares, like showing up at school to take an exam for a class I never attended. I dunno, I'm just spitballing here.

We walked into the school and went directly to our classroom. It was normal, too normal. I should have known she had something up her sleeve.

Then, when we were all turning in our homework after morning announcements, Bronnie clutched my arm as she walked by my desk. She wrapped grabbed her arms around her stomach and made the most horrible groaning sound I've ever heard come out of a human being. She sounded like a farm animal caught in a trap.

Mrs. Andrews rushed over in a flurry, her cashmere shawl flowing behind her like a cape. She threaded her way through our classmates who in turn were desperate to get away from

Bronnie, should she vomit or pop out an alien or something.

Mrs. Andrews held Bronnie's arm and touched her forehead. I caught a glimpse of a blue gecko tattoo on our teacher's upper arm that she had managed to keep hidden until today. It distracted me and then Bronnie groaned again.

"Oh my dear, are you alright?" Our teacher helped her to a chair.

Bronnie held on to Mrs. Andrews for support and let out a slightly less obnoxious whimper. "I'm...I'm not entirely sure." She managed to whisper.

My eyes rolled so far back into my head I could see my own brain. She was totally faking. I knew it, but no one else did.

Mrs. Andrews knelt down and looked into Bronnie's eyes which were bloodshot and surrounded by dark circles. "It looks to me like you aren't quite well enough for school yet. We had better get you to the nurse. I'll get Mr. Carter from next door to keep an eye on the class and then we will go down to the office together."

Sucking in a breath and straightening her back just enough to seem believable, Bronnie exhaled. "No. There is no need for that, I can manage." Our teacher was about to argue, but Bronnie saw this coming and said, "The pain seems to have passed. I'm sure I'll be fine to make it there by myself. Maybe, if another student could walk with me, just in case." She fluttered her eyes in my direction.

Well, hell.

Mrs. Andrews glanced around at the class, which had rapidly become unruly and came to the obvious conclusion leaving them unsupervised was a bad idea. As the only student still seated and Bronnie's closest friend, our teacher's eyes settled on me. "Sean, please accompany Bronwyn down to the nurse's office. Come back when she is settled. No rush."

The very instant our classroom door closed behind us Bronnie stood erect and began to speed walk down the hall just as she had done earlier in the year with Jamie Caldwell and me in tow. I tried to keep up, half wanting to strangle her for what she had just pulled in class..

We would have to have a talk.

Oh my god, I sound like my father.

The same broad counter was there, bisecting the room lengthwise to separate the waiting chairs from the administration desks where two school office managers were hard at work. One of them was Miss Faraday. Her blonde hair was cropped close to her head so it emphasized her punk rock glasses. With a purple knitted shawl over her shoulders, she looked like Tweetie Bird's Granny went through a time warp.

Miss Faraday glanced up from her work and smiled at us brightly. "Hello,

Bronnie and Sean. Is there something we can help you with?"

I had planned to immediately distance myself from whatever Bronnie was cooking up, but before I could open my mouth, the other school secretary excused herself and left through the side door to the restroom.

This was probably lucky for both her and for us since she would have been an innocent bystander in the coming onslaught that began with Bronnie innocently saying, "I'd like to speak with you, Miss Faraday."

"Of course. Whatever about, Bronnie?" She said, taking a sip from her water bottle.

I tried to interject as best I could, "I have nothing to do with this, Miss Faraday...I"

"We need to speak to you about Bethany Grieves." Bronnie cut me off.

At the mention of her name, Miss Faraday's face turned ashen and she dropped the water bottle. It landed on her keyboard, then the desk, then hit the floor with a thud and rolled slowly along the tile coming to a final stop by the radiator.

The main thought I had, watching it roll, was being thankful that she had already put the top back on the bottle. It would have been one heck of a mess otherwise.

Miss Faraday and Bronnie, however, were locked in each other's gaze.

The principal, Mrs. Duncan, apparently sensed something was afoot, because she poked her perfectly coiffed head out of her office, her fingernails clicking on the doorway as she did.

"Jennifer, is everything ok out here?" Mrs. Duncan inquired, with more warmth than I had ever seen her show her students.

Miss Faraday sat in shocked silence. Our principal stepped out of her office to get a better look at the situation and immediately saw us. She took one look at Bronnie and exhaled as though she were preparing. (I stood there waving my hands at my waist so she could see I wanted no part of this.)

Mrs. Duncan narrowed her gaze and crossed her arms. "Is this about what I think it is about, Jennifer?" Even though her question was directed at her admin, she kept her eyes locked on Bronnie. Her tone was even, not angry.

Miss Faraday managed a nod in response.

Our principal pushed the door to her office wide open and said with more exasperation than authority "You all had better come in here."

I tried to stay behind, but she reiterated, "All." So much for distancing myself.

The three of us filed into the side office just as the other secretary was emerging from the lavatory. She either had uncanny timing or a tremendous amount of experience of leaving awkward situations at just the right time.

Our principal motioned for us to sit down into two ancient and cracked leather guest chairs that were facing her desk. She sat down in her big swivel office chair while Miss Faraday stood behind her, her shawl wrapped tightly around her shoulders. Her face was gradually regaining its color, her shock turning to what appeared to be a mix of anger and fear. I whispered to Bronnie to tread carefully.

Before we were seated, Mrs. Duncan started speaking. "Even though this, like so many other things is probably none of your business, how can we help you today Miss Browne?"

Perhaps Bronnie was meant to be deterred by the way our principal opened the proceedings, but she wasn't. "I was just wondering why one of our school secretaries, and apparently our principal, is faking the existence of a student."

"Ah." Mrs. Duncan picked up a stack of papers. We watched quietly as she straightened them and slid them into a waiting file folder.

Finally, Miss Faraday took a step forward and leaned down. "We may as well tell them, Meredith."

She laid a gentle hand on Miss Faraday's arm. "Jennifer, you don't have to tell them anything."

"May as well." She let show a cautious smile. "Miss Browne doesn't

strike me as the type of girl to leave
unanswered questions alone. And it
might feel good to talk about this in
the open after so many years."

Her change of demeanor made me
relax. It was then I realized that I had
been clenching my hands and jaw ever
since we had left the classroom.

"So Bronnie," Miss Faraday said, as
she came around to the front of the
desk and leaned against it, "what
exactly have you figured out?"

I thought Bronnie would jump at the
chance to put on a smug face and
rattle off the clues she had found, but
she didn't. There was something going
on in her head, a puzzle still to be
worked out. She was still searching.

Bronnie answered the question anyway, "There were a few clues. I noticed one too many pieces of art on the walls, a skip in the student ID numbers at lunch, photos of a student no one recognized in the newspaper. The main giveaway, however, I found was at the holiday concert."

Miss Faraday nodded, "The extra name added to the winter concert program. Yes, that was obvious, wasn't it."

Bronnie shrugged, "I might have overlooked it, if I hadn't already been curious."

Mrs. Duncan chuffed. She caught my eye and asked me, "What part did you have to play in all of this, Mr.

Watkins. Or are you just an innocent bystander."

It didn't appear that we were in any trouble, but you never knew when adults were laying a trap for you. "Well, Bronnie noticed most of the clues. I just kind of helped out with research."

Bronnie jumped in, "He is a good sounding board. I mean, a good companion. A friend. But it was my idea to come here today."

"Yes, I gathered that." Mrs. Duncan said.

I exhaled a small sigh of relief.

Bronnie began "When we realized that it was likely Miss Faraday was the one helping to fake Bethany's enrollment at the schools..."

"Schools?" Jennifer replied. "You know about the other ones?"

"Yes, all of them, since Kindergarten." Bronnie replied. "So we have the 'who', 'when' and the 'where' questions answered."

Miss Faraday nodded.

Bronnie continued. "Since you run the graphic arts and photography club, I'm assuming your hobby accounts for the 'how'."

Miss Faraday spoke. "So you figured the fastest way to find out 'why' was to come directly to ask me."

My friend nodded this time. "I'm sorry to be so abrupt, but am in a bit of a time crunch."

Miss Faraday seemed to find her courage. "Bethany's father,"

"Emmanuel Grieves." I interjected.

The secretary bristled at the mention of his name. "Yes, Emmanuel Grieves, Bethany's father, is not a nice man. He is brutal and sadistic."

Bronnie said, with very little emotion, "So the arrest warrant for assault and battery, that was for domestic abuse."

There was a deep exhale, almost in unison, from both of the older women. "It was."

The hairs on my arms were standing straight up. All of my bad dreams from the night before somehow didn't seem so silly anymore. I opened my mouth slowly. "So Bethany's dad was abusive?"

Miss Faraday cracked her knuckles, one by one, but her voice was shaky. "Yes," she managed, "the kind of person nightmares are made of."

She walked over to the window and stared out at the gray sky, which seemed to reflect the mood in the office.

"Elizabeth, Bethany's mom, was my best friend all through school. We did everything together. We were on the same swim teams, in a lot of the same classes. When she met Emmanuel, or Manny as she called him, our friendship changed. We didn't see each other anymore. No movies, no trips to the mall, no more late nights with friends."

She abruptly walked over to the corner of the room. I noticed a small refrigerator humming away under a table. She took out a water bottle and offered some around the room. Mrs. Duncan accepted one, but Bronnie and I didn't move. I was afraid any word from us might break the spell and she would stop talking.

Miss Faraday continued, "I never liked him, not even from the start. She was a senior in high school and he was older, a lot older. But it wasn't just my preference, Elizabeth changed right in front of my eyes. She had planned to go into the Navy after night school. She wanted to be a rescue diver, she loved the ocean. We used to swim, right out there."

She pointed out of the window towards the sound beyond the harbor.

"We'd swim to the island and back, dodging lobster boats. But something changed when she met Manny."

Miss Faraday took a long drink of water, walking around the room as she did, fiddling with random things on shelves. "Little by little he took her away from us, and us away from her dreams. Then, just before the end of senior year, she announced she wasn't going to college, or the academy. She was getting married." It seemed her sadness got the better of her, "Married to that monster." The school secretary's voice cracked and she stopped.

Mrs. Duncan stood up to offer her chair to Miss Faraday. Then she stood straight and came to the front of the desk. "This is a small town, Bronnie...Sean. Even in a small town, sometimes it is possible to keep secrets. Elizabeth gave birth to Bethany that summer after high school. Her family disowned her, which Manny probably expected. Elizabeth and her daughter became dependent entirely upon him and he knew it. Her isolation from the rest of the world was complete. She had no job, no money, no family support, and a child to care for."

Bronnie spoke cautiously. "Is that when he started abusing her?"

Our principal's lifted her head so she gazed down at us. "Your parents seem like nice people. Yours too, Sean, are they? Are they nice people?"

"Yes," I answered, with some unintentional confusion in my tone, "They are."

Mrs. Duncan's eyes, her whole demeanor turned cold. Like someone had poured liquid nitrogen over her while she stood in front of us. "Emmanuel Grieves is not a nice person. He is a gaslighter, a schemer. He is the epitome of evil."

"What is a gaslighter?" I asked.

Bronnie answered for the adults. "A psychological manipulator, they do terrible things then makes the victim think it was their own fault." Bronnie unlocked her gaze from Mrs. Duncan and looked at Miss Faraday. "When did you find out? About the abuse, I mean."

Jennifer took a deep breath. "I did some substitute teaching over at Cliffside elementary one day. Bethany was in my class, I knew exactly who she was and was so happy to see her. She had her mom's bright eyes and beautiful curly hair. I hadn't seen her since she was born and even then, only briefly." She looked above our heads, watching the seconds tick on the principal's clock. "Bethany was balancing on one of the logs that borders the playground. She slipped, banging her elbow and hip as she fell down. We took her into the nurse's office and needed to lift her shirt to check where she had fallen. It was then we saw bruises all over her arms, on her back. Even her long, curly hair was covering marks on her neck, like she had been choked."

My friend sucked in air. I saw anger boiling in her usually calm face. "So you called the police. You called Officer De La Rosa, right?"

This deduction snapped Miss Faraday out of her trance. "Yes. Officer De La Rosa was the first officer to respond. He is the main police liaison for the schools."

Mrs. Duncan interjected. She spoke quickly. "This wasn't the first time the police had been called on Manny, but it was the first time outsiders had gotten involved. And officer De La Rosa wasn't going to sweep it under the rug like some other beat cops had. It wasn't easy, but we finally convinced

Elizabeth to press charges and to leave him. We eventually found them a place to stay at a local women's shelter."

Bronnie closed her eyes, fluttered her fingers in the air, then opened them again. "I can't believe I missed it in the yearbook. You were Vice Principal at the school, at Cliffside."

Mrs. Duncan nodded and turned to the school secretary who was now holding her face in her hands and sobbing quietly. "I don't think Elizabeth would have done it, would have left him, if Jennifer had not been the one to find out. Having her best friend there to help, to lean on. It must have been what gave her the courage to finally leave him. She knew she was no longer alone."

We sat in silence. Bronnie's face like an angry mask, her hands clenched, tears were forming in her eyes. My mind was still grappling with the unfathomable reality that someone could abuse a helpless child.

Assault and battery, such legal and cold sounding words for such a horrible act.

Bronnie's thoughts must have been following mine. "What happened next?"

"They never got very far. It started simple enough, but as soon as the first arrest warrant was issued, Emmanuel disappeared."

"Wait. What?" I blurted out. "He isn't in jail?"

"Arrest warrant, no arrest record," Bronnie said calmly and slowly. "And at this point, if he were to show again, the likelihood of convicting him on 7 year old charges is probably slim. Even if they are felonies."

Mrs. Duncan let a thin smile cross her lips, as though she were showing some pride in Bronnie. "I'm not sure what luck anyone would have convicting him, especially..."

Bronnie glanced between Miss Faraday and Mrs. Duncan, "Especially since Elizabeth and Bethany Grieves wouldn't be testifying at his trial."

I felt like my ears perked up like a dog. "What do you mean they wouldn't testify. You said yourself they had agreed to press charges."

"That's just it," Bronnie said. "They had agreed to press charges, not only on assault but child abuse as well. Then Mr. Grieves skipped town. He disappeared, leaving Mrs..."

Miss Faraday interjected. "He had always threatened to take Bethany away. Always said that Elizabeth would never be able to leave him. Before the police were called that time, we would see him watching Bethany. He would follow them home from school. He was always there, stalking them, his own family." She shuddered.

"So you helped them disappear." Bronnie hinted.

"Not at first." Miss Faraday answered. "Elizabeth wanted to do it on her own, with help from the shelter, of course. But she slipped up and he found her. Only by her own resourcefulness was she able to escape a second time."

Bronnie inhaled deeply. "You helped her after that."

Jennifer nodded. "She was broke. It wasn't easy, trying to raise a kid as a single mom with no higher education, no experience. And to do it all under the radar. So yes, I made some phone calls."

"Nothing illegal about it, really." Mrs. Duncan pre-empted. "He disappeared first, on his own to avoid a trial. Elizabeth got her divorce and full custody. She took the opportunity to get away."

We sat in silence for what seemed like an eternity. Finally, I spoke just to break the tension. "So why are you pretending that Bethany Grieves goes to school here."

Bronnie interjected. "It is a false trail, isn't it?"

Miss Faraday was lost in thought, but Mrs. Duncan gave the slightest of nods.

"What?" I said.

My friend continued. "A false trail. You see, if Bethany disappears entirely, he would know they took off and would search for them. But, if there is evidence of her here, he will stay here. He will waste his time in this area trying to track her down, leaving the real mother and daughter free to get away. So, Miss Faraday was using her position as a school employee floater to create false Bethany Grieves throughout the school system. All in the hopes of letting Elizabeth leave without being noticed."

Mrs. Duncan said, "And it has worked so far. I assume we can trust both of you to keep this very important secret." Her tone had a kind of finality that, had I been younger, might have made me wet my pants. "It isn't an exaggeration to say that lives depend upon it."

Bronnie nodded thoughtfully. "Miss Faraday, has he ever approached you, directly I mean?"

"Once. Years ago. But I keep myself pretty well armed. Besides, he would want to grab Bethany and run, not open a new can of worms with me. Honestly, I think it must be getting

more difficult to keep Manny convinced.
We can leave evidence lying around,
but at the end of the day, Bethany is
not here."

Mrs. Duncan stood straight.
"Bronnie, Sean, you must let us know if
you have seen anything or anyone who
may be suspicious. Mr. Grieves is a
dangerous man, this situation is not to
be taken lightly."

Bronnie quickly asked, "What does
Emmanuel Grieves look like?"

"I haven't seen him in a long while.
He was nice enough looking man, a
little taller than I am. He had dark
brown hair that he wore a long on top
and slicked back. Manny always was a
good dresser. Oh, he had blue eyes and
a scar on his upper lip."

Before I could say anything, Bronnie blurted out, "We'll keep an eye out." She stood up abruptly.

My friend must have sensed some tension because as she stood to leave, she casually said "I understand why Miss Faraday would want to get involved and help her friends...but why would you, Mrs. Duncan."

Mrs. Duncan's countenance had not changed, but she said kindly, "Maybe the same reason Sean is here with you. We should always try to help our friends."

With that cryptic answer, we were ushered out of the office and made our way back to our class. Halfway down the hall, around the place where Bronnie had noticed the missing artwork at Christmas, she spoke softly. "You know, he will find her, eventually."

I nodded. "After so many years and not seeing her. He has to be suspicious."

She didn't say another word to anyone the rest of the day.

Chapter 9

The next morning, on the bus, Bronnie was a bundle of nerves. She bounced in her seat and patted the green vinyl next to her.

Of course, I was wary. "What's up?" I said.

"I've got the solution." Bronnie said, "I've figured it out."

My expression must have been straight confusion. "Figured what out? The thing with Bethany? I know, I was there, remember?"

"Not that, silly," she whispered. "I know what has to be done. I'll need your help, though."

I took a deep breath and let it out. So far in hanging out with Bronnie, I'd barely managed to avoid getting arrested, grounded and suspended. Who knew how long my luck would last.

On the other hand, this was the most excitement I'd ever had. Maybe the most I ever would have. Being with her was like living inside of a detective movie.

It occurred to me, from this point on, I had to either end our friendship or make a final decision quit second-guessing Bronnie. I could either support my friend and consequently this girl Bethany or I could shut them both out and pretend the predicament had nothing to do with me.

The right decision was obvious.

"What do you need?" I asked.

Bronnie looked relieved. "I need you to get Matt De La Rosa to sit with us at lunch, or at the very least, talk with us at in study hall."

It may not seem like the hardest task in the world, but getting a middle school kid to change their normal routine at lunch or study hall would be like getting your teacher to give up teaching and play movies all day. "Ok, why can't you ask him."

Bronnie leaned away from me in surprise. "Because he likes you better, everyone does. I'm sort of...what's the word?"

"Overwhelming." The word had left my lips before I could stop it, immediately I regretted saying it.

My friend was not offended though, "Overwhelming, right." She jotted notes on a little pad and slid it into her backpack. She was silent for the rest of the journey to school.

As we pulled into the town, the bus drove by some of the dilapidated apartments lining the inner harbor. Probably stately row houses years ago, now they were a mess of peeling white paint and crooked porches. Dad had said it was where a lot of the itinerant and seasonal workers lived. Rent was cheap and sometimes subsidized by the local companies who needed the employees to do undesirable jobs like gut fish or pick lobster meat.

I recognized a young girl from days I helped my dad at the free clinic in town. She was probably not beyond third grade, walking by herself up the hill to school, lugging a torn princess backpack. The rest of her body was almost completely swallowed up by a bright purple down parka.

Bronnie's parka.

"Hey, that girl..." I pointed her out, but Bronnie only glanced at the kid and looked away.

As it turned out, getting Matt to sit with us at lunch was easier than expected. He gotten into a heated argument with his best friend about the underrated merits of independent comic book companies and consequently they weren't on speaking terms. Also, Bronnie had brought brownies to share.

Preparation is key.

"Thank you for sitting with us, Matt." She said, rather formally.

He simply nodded a reply, which was probably best because his mouth was full of chocolate brownie mush.

"I know it is generally for the younger grades, but are you planning to attend the movie night at school?" She continued. Matt shrugged, he was a man of few words, apparently.

Bronnie looked at me, her eyes pleading for support. I wrinkled my eyebrows, to silently explain that I was not exactly sure what she wanted me to do. She kicked me under the table.

"What she means," I said, "is do you usually go to the movie nights?"

Matt nodded this time. "Yeah, mom and dad usually make it a date night, if dad doesn't have to work. I'm not trusted at home alone."

"Why aren't you..." I started to ask but Bronnie interrupted.

"Does he have to work this time?"

I don't know why, but I put my hand on her arm to steady her.

He took a big drink of milk and reached for another brownie, "Prolly not, he doesn't pull night shifts much anymore. And I heard mom hinting about going out for sushi."

"Excellent." Bronnie smiled and finally eased back on the bench. "You'll have to sit with us, I'll bring more food."

Matt seemed to enjoy this suggestion. "Cool." He mumbled. I noticed he had consumed three brownies, was working on a fourth and had left his lunch untouched.

I was dying to ask Bronnie why it was such a big deal to have Matt sit with us, especially since it was just a simple question of the movie night two days from now. We wandered out to the open area after eating, but she wasn't talking much. She was deep in thought, staring through the now leafless trees that lined the soccer fields and out to the harbor.

"What is going on with you?" I blurted out, surprised at how angry I sounded. Her eyes widened, but she didn't answer and tried to look away. I continued, "You've been acting even weirder than usual. Normally it is cool, I mean, I'm used to it. But you are scaring me now."

"Why should my being quiet scare you?" She asked, her hands had moved to her hips, but she didn't seem to be confronting me.

"Because I at least know you well enough to tell when you are up to something, and you are definitely up to something." I crossed my arms and looked at her directly. Just then the bell rang, but I touched her arm so she couldn't sneak away.

Finally, Bronnie exhaled deeply and relented. "I'm just trying to figure out one last piece of the puzzle, it is bothering me. I wondered if Matt's dad could help out, that is all. If Officer De La Rosa will be picking him up at movie night, it makes it easier to speak with him." She took her hands off of her hips, "Is that ok with you?"

I felt like she let the air out of my balloon, but her answer did put me at ease. "Ok." We started walking back to the building. "That makes sense. He was the officer in charge of the case all of those years ago."

"Right." She responded, and said nothing else as we entered the school.

On the bus home, Bronnie was quiet again. The sun glinted off of her curls and made them look lighter than usual.

That night over dinner of Thai drunken noodles and bright orange iced tea, I brought up the subject of Bronnie and her strange behavior to my parents. "She's quiet." I continued, after having given them a rundown of the day. "More quiet than usual."

My mom shrugged at first. "It must be exhausting, having a mind like hers. Whenever I've seen her it is like she is constantly working out a problem and making connections. Maybe she is just needs some downtime."

"Maybe." I said.

Dad chimed in, "Anything else?"

How could I tell them my concerns without divulging the entire Bethany Grieves investigation we'd been working on. Without mentioning the hacking of computers, or the search for a dangerous known fugitive, not to mention the trips to the principal's office.

"Besides being distant?" I said. "Well, she's getting forgetful. She's on her third new coat and the fourth sweatshirt this year."

"She could just be preoccupied. Brilliant people are usually less concerned with the every day." Dad stroked his non-existent beard in thought. "Otherwise, is everything ok at home? Could she be in any danger."

I almost spit out my iced tea. "Bronnie? In danger. I doubt it."

Mom nodded, "She is rather...formidable, isn't she?"

Dad clarified his point, "I'm just saying that when a person undergoes something traumatic or painful, they rarely talk about it. Usually, the signs manifest in other ways. Poor grades, withdrawing from social situations, becoming a bully, these are all classic signs of abuse."

I shivered at the suggestion, but thinking of Bethany, not Bronnie. And then of course thinking of our school bully, Pokeyfinger and what his home life must be like. "No, I don't think that is it."

"Well good," Dad said. "I like Bronnie and her parents seem like nice folks. It would be fun to see more of them."

"Oh! Speaking of," I said and swallowed a mouthful of noodles before talking any more. Friday night is movie night at school. Can I go?"

"Sure." My Mom said. "Your dad and I were planning on doing some light vandalism that night anyway."

"I'm in," Dad played along. "The police will never suspect us to be the culprits. We are entirely too boring."

"My friend Matt's dad is the police." I laughed.

"Then we will wear gloves." Mom smiled.

I turned to Dad. "That graffiti will be terrible, with your doctor's handwriting and all. No one will be able to understand it."

"Art isn't meant to be understood."

Mom giggled, "No, but your prescriptions are."

"Touché." Dad said and then stole a sip of my iced tea.

Movie night came about with more anticipation than you would think a two year old movie and stale popcorn would warrant. Students and their families lined up at the main doors next to the cafeteria and got signed in one by one. Mom handed me a name tag as though I were a kindergartener and waited with me until Bronnie and Matt arrived.

Officer De La Rosa arrived out of uniform but still intimidating with his crew cut and military stance. He tried to act casually as I introduced him to my mother.

Bronnie arrived introduced her parents and shook his hand, but didn't ask him any of the questions she told me she had planned. Perhaps she would wait until after the movie. She still wasn't making much eye contact with me.

Mostly she stared out of the windows into the parking lot.

Our parents all decided that a triple date night at the sushi bar was in order causing Matt, Bronnie and me to groan in unison.

Eventually we were herded into the cafeteria by a few teachers and volunteer parents. Each of us carrying blankets and pillows to use on the cold tile floor.

The movie showing was one I had seen it about twelve times before. It straddled the gray line between something to keep the kindergarteners entertained and yet not drive away the older students. Mostly the upper school kids sat in the back, whispered and played card games. Bronnie sat ramrod straight through the entire picture and barely acknowledged Matt except to pass him food.

About two hours later, the film ended. Parents overseeing the event wandered in to help sweep up popcorn and fold wayward blankets. My mom, Mrs. Browne, and officer De La Rosa were chatting with a group of parents near the doors. Judging by his hand gestures he was recounting the Root

Beer Incident to the amusement of our mothers. Matt licked the last of the chocolate from his fingertips.

Man, that kid could put away brownies.

Bronnie's mom was laughing so hard she had tears streaming down her face when our parents made it over to our side. "So where is Bronnie?" My mom said. "I'd love to congratulate her on fine detective work."

I turned around to gesture behind my back. "She's right here..." My stomach dropped. Bronnie wasn't there.

The scene in the cafeteria was innocent enough but in the pit of my stomach I knew there was something off.

"She isn't here." I turned my head in every direction. "She was right here. Right here!" I pointed at the floor next to my foot.

"I'm sure she just went to the restroom." My mom said. She instinctively touched Mrs. Browne's arm, though.

We frantically searched the room. It was clearing out of kids, but there were still plenty people around. Bronnie's red coat was gone, but the rest of her things were still on the floor. Her phone, bag, pillow, and blanket all still neatly laid out where they had been next to mine. Our principal, who had been in charge of the parent volunteers for the event came over to our group. I looked at her with wide eyes.

"Is anything wrong, Sean?" She asked. "You look a little flustered."

My mom spoke and tried her best to sound calm "It appears that we have misplaced Bronnie. Have you seen her?"

Mrs. Duncan furrowed her brow, "Not since she came for popcorn midway through the film. I've been at the door for pickup and didn't see her go. Is it possible she went to the restroom?"

Officer De La Rosa instinctively changed his posture from easygoing dad to all business police officer. I noticed my mom mimic his stance. "What was she wearing?" he asked.

Her mom faltered, "She had a purple, I mean no, she lost that..." and then she trailed off. Her head was turning frantically now and she began to wring the bottom of her jacket in her hands. "Oh god, what was she wearing."

I spoke up with more fortitude than I would have thought possible, given the circumstances. "She has a bright red wood coat, with a hood. Under that she had a green corduroy blazer, white polo shirt, blue jeans and a pair of penny loafers. Her hair was back in a green headband and she had a blue wristwatch on her hand."

Bronnie must have been rubbing off on me, because all of the adults (and even Matt in his brownie glory) gaped at me.

Mrs. Duncan locked eyes with me. "You don't think."

"Mr. Grieves." I whispered.

At that sound of the name, Officer De La Rosa set his jaw and yelled with a voice so loud and deep that it echoed through the halls and caused the hairs on my arms to stand on end, "Put the school on lockdown. Now!" He whipped out his cell phone and dialed frantically.

Mrs. Browne stood staring at the room like a deer in headlights. A tear fluttered down her cheek. She called out Bronnie's name repeatedly; her voice seemed to catch on the word. It occurred to me then that her personality was so entirely unlike Bronnie's. Her fear for her daughter showing through in every way it could.

My mom took my cell phone out of my hand. "I need to call your dad, he is waiting with Mr. Browne in the parking lot." She clicked the home button and glanced at the display. "Sean, what is this?"

I looked at the screen. "That's strange," I said, "there is an alarm going off. A proximity alarm, but I don't recognize the app."

I handed it to Officer De La Rosa, who peered at it with Mrs. Browne. "Some kind of GPS tracking function." He said.

"Pardon?" Mrs. Browne's eyes went wide and she snatched the phone. "That her GPS app, we used that when she was little. Just in case she ever got lost. Why would..."

I thought for a split second, the wristwatch. "Quick. What does it look like? The tag?"

Mrs. Browne's was shaking. "Just a black, plastic tag. About the size of a quarter. It went into a rubber wristband."

"A blue wristband! Mr. Grieves!" I yelled and took the phone back from Mrs. Browne, which was a move sure to get me grounded. "Bronnie knew he would try to take her. She wants us to track her!"

My mom looked at me, the phone, Mrs. Duncan and a just arrived Miss Faraday. "You keep saying that. Who is this Mr. Grieves? Will someone please explain to me what the hell is going on?"

"Not now," I yelled. My heart was pumping and my adrenaline was surging. I tried to stay focused, scanning the blinking dot on the phone and the hallway. "There!!" I pointed, towards the back of the school near the library. "That way!" I broke into a run leaving my bag and all of the adults in my wake.

If you left the cafeteria and turned right you could walk the length of the school, and then exit the building through a set of doors on the opposite end of the library. It was a straight shot. But I was almost positive the doors to the library itself would be closed, shutting down my potential exit there.

So, halfway down the hall, just passed the restrooms, I turned left and ducked out of a side door. It was one that was used primarily during recess. The sidewalk from it led to picnic tables and the basketball court near the playground.

I noticed when pushing through the doors to the outside, that no alarm sounded like it should have. Especially with the school on lock down, it shouldn't have opened at all.

The rear of the school was not well lit at night. As I reached the far side of the basketball courts, I saw two shapes barely visible in the mist and moonlight. They were walking quietly past the playground, towards the sidewalk which led to a neighborhood behind the school. If they made it through the trees, they would be on the street. A street leading past the harbor and directly to the highway. Mr. Grieves probably had a car waiting for a fast getaway. Even though Bronnie had on her **GPS** tag, I was 100% sure we didn't want her getting going anywhere with that psycho.

I had to get their attention, to get them to stop walking, without having him hurt her. It may have been a terrible decision, but I shouted "Manny Grieves, freeze!"

Not one of my more creative moments, but it worked. The two figures abruptly stopped under a dim streetlight just on our side of the tree line. Their backs were still facing us and mist in the air swirled around their figures making me feel like they might disappear into the fog at any moment.

Officer De La Rosa caught up with me, lowering his phone to his waist. "Turn around, no sudden moves." He didn't yell but spoke loudly and with authority. Even though he was not in uniform and carried no gun that I could see, the tone of his voice commanded obedience from everyone. Everyone except Manny Grieves. That ahole didn't move.

Bronnie didn't move either. As we inched closer, we could see Manny's right arm on Bronnie's shoulder and his left hand lower in front. He was holding something in that hand and moved it closer to my friend. From the distance, I couldn't see what it was.

The **GPS** tracker was still flashing on the phone in my hand. I slid it into my pocket so Manny wouldn't notice. If they got away, it was all we had to find her.

Officer De La Rosa spoke again, this time with more compassion. "We just want to talk."

The two finally turned to face us. Mr. Grieves' voice was cold and calm. "Talk about what." It wasn't a question.

Mrs. Browne was sobbing. Her hands continued to twist her clothes. "Please, please, let her go."

"Now why the hell would I do that?" He inched a step back, still holding Bronnie's shoulder.

"There's no reason for you to take her, Manny. She is innocent. Just let her go and walk away." The police officer matched him for calm, but not coldness.

"Please." Mrs. Browne pleaded. "Don't take my little girl."

Mr. Grieves leaned his head forward, trying to get a better look at us in the dim light. He stopped inching backward. I thought it was probably Mrs. Browne's accent giving him pause. She wouldn't have sounded at all like Elizabeth. With her small stature and hijab, even in the dark, he should have been able to tell she was not his ex-wife. I hoped it might confuse him long enough to buy us some time.

He shook his head and held Bronnie's shoulder tighter. "She's my girl. Mine. I told you not to take her from me. I told you that you would pay if you did."

Mrs. Browne's sobs stuck in her throat.

Officer De La Rosa started to speak, but I knew it would terrible for us if Mr. Grieves discovered that the little girl with him was not his daughter. Who knew what he would do? If he could be so cruel to the people closest to him, to his own flesh and blood, what would he do to Bronnie?

I yelled out before anyone else could. "We know you want Bethany.

We know you've been looking for her. You can't take her away like this. The police will find you."

Mrs. Browne glanced at me in confusion. I put my hand on her arm to steady her.

The officer next to me sucked in some air, apparently putting the pieces together on his own. "You drove them away, Manny." He yelled. "You beat your own daughter, your own wife. What did you expect?"

"What did I expect?" Mr. Grieves shouted, then cackled. There was no other word for it, he cackled like a damn psycho. Jerking Bronnie with him, he took another step back towards the trees. They were only a few feet from the darkness, we hadn't moved forward at all.

We could hear him sucking in air all the way across the playground. I'd seen enough movies to know he was about to start his monologue. Which was fine with me, we needed the time.

"I expected, my wife and child, to be obedient, like they were supposed to! Isn't that what wedding vows say, to honor and obey. Doesn't the bible say they should submit to me in all things?"

I resisted the urge to make gagging noises.

Manny continued. "I expected them to treat me with honor and respect! All I got was their fear and their hatred!" He let out another cold, sinister laugh. "But... after all of this...I suppose I can live with fear and hatred."

He jerked Bronnie's shoulder. "Isn't that right, Bethany?" He practically spat the name.

Mrs. Browne let out a whimper and fell to her knees. Bronnie's tilted her ear towards the bushes, then calmly lifted her head to glare at the man next to her.

She spoke clearly and calmly. "There are so many things wrong with what you just said. But the main problem is, I'm not Bethany."

In the pale light, I saw a flash of confusion cross Manny's face and his left hand dropped slightly. Whatever was in that hand was no longer pointing at Bronnie, but at the ground.

In that split second Bronnie made a move so fast I could barely see what happened. She had grabbed her captor's left wrist, wrenched it, and spun around. When her move was finished, she was on the opposite side behind him. Manny's hand was now empty, held behind his back and bent in an unnatural and apparently a very painful position.

At that exact moment, to my complete astonishment, someone leapt from the trees on side where Bronnie had been standing a second before. Wielding what appeared to be a tree branch, they swung it hard like a baseball bat and caught Manny directly under the chin.

He immediately began to crumple. Bronnie released his wrist and watched him collapse first at the knees, then hips, and then lastly his torso pitched forward so that his face landed with a smack onto the concrete. He immediately began to snore; his arms limp at the sides and his butt sticking up in the air at a most unattractive angle.

It was a beautiful sight.

I wished I had thought to take a picture of it. There they were, standing over the unconscious villain in triumph. My mom tossed the tree branch aside and wrapped her arm around Bronnie.

I told you she was like a ninja.

Mrs. Browne finally realized what had happened and then broke into a full run, with the rest of us trailing in her wake. She practically tackled Bronnie in relief, taking a few well earned kicks at Manny's sleeping body while we pretended not to notice.

I hugged my mom around the waist as we wandered our way back to the building.

Bronnie nodded an acknowledgment to my mother. "Thank you, Mrs. Watkins."

My mom returned the tone and nod "It was my distinct pleasure, Miss Browne."

Chapter 10

In the real world, the justice system is not as quick and clean as it seems on television. Court cases are not handled in 45 minutes, with enough time for commercial breaks. The bad guy doesn't always confess when he is cornered. And sometimes really terrible things happen to really good people.

So I suddenly felt exhausted and not very optimistic as Bronnie and I sat in the back of my mom's car watching the night's scene unfold around us.

All of the families that had arrived for movie night had finally gone home.

Bronnie's parents held each other tightly, answering a detective's questions. Mr. Browne watched with cold, and frankly terrifying eyes, as Manny Grieves half conscious body was loaded into an ambulance (under police guard of course).

Matt De La Rosa leaned on his dad, nearly asleep on his feet, probably coming down off of another brownie-induced sugar high.

There was a knock on our window, we both turned to see Miss Faraday and Mrs. Duncan peering through the glass. I pressed the button to lower it.

Miss Faraday was not doing a very good job of suppressing a smile.

Mrs. Duncan, by contrast, was wearing a frown and had her arms crossed. "Would you two please be so kind as to explain yourselves?"

I really had no idea how to respond. Mrs. Duncan had witnessed the entire part I had to play including, but not limited to, my rude comments, phone snatching and mad dash out of the cafeteria.

Bronnie looked at her with all of the pretended innocence she could muster. "It is just that...well...I thought I had seen Mr. Grieves around the school. At the winter concert and such and..." She usually spoke with such confidence that this pretense of not knowing what to say was almost laughable.

"And what?" Mrs. Duncan pressed.

"And, well, I just worried that he might have been thinking I was Bethany.

Since we sort of looked alike." She gently touched the blue band on her wrist. "So I started wearing my old GPS tag, just in case. And I installed the app on my parents' and Sean's phones.

She and Mrs. Duncan proceeded to have a staring contest. (My money was on Bronnie.)

Miss Faraday finally came forward and gently nudged Mrs. Duncan out of the doorway. "Well, we are just glad that you aren't hurt. It was a dangerous situation to be in, you were very brave." She reached to Bronnie and squeezed her hand, tears welling in her eyes.

Bronnie looked quickly away, keeping her gaze on the windshield, I thought I saw a tear roll down her cheek. "Thank you for the compliment."

I closed the window against the cold. Bronnie and I observed the night through the windshield.

"You wore the band, just in case?" I said.

She shrugged.

"Lightened your hair?" I ventured.

"Blonde highlights, $6.99 hidden from my mum under the bread in our shopping trolley." She narrowed her gaze as the ambulance doors shut.

I gave the faintest smile and said softly. "And your new blue eyes."

Now Bronnie was exuding pure confidence, "Contacts ordered online from a costume company. It took me an hour to get them in the first day I wore them. Damned uncomfortable." She shuddered slightly.

I leaned in closer. "Those pictures on your laptop were of him, weren't they. Of Manny. He was stalking you. That is why you installed the cameras instead of just the mirrors." She didn't answer me, so I sighed. "You should have called the police Bronnie. You should have at least told Matt's dad."

Her eyes welled up and she wiped away the tears angrily with the arm of her coat. "Seven years Sean. That is how old those charges against him were. Bethany was never going to be safe, never going to be free of him even if they did catch him."

She turned to me and forced a smile. "Kidnapping, especially with a firearm, however is also a felony. One which carries a minimum ten year prison sentence in our state. And, technically he didn't even need to make me leave with him to qualify as a kidnapper. So in my defense, I hand't really planned to let it go that far."

I stared at her.

She pointed to the building. "The mystery now is to find out how he managed to bypass the locks and alarms on the school doors."

"Oh great." I rubbed my temples. "Another mystery."

Bronnie shivered and put her hands in her pockets.

What I don't understand," I said, turning to face her, "is why, after coming to the winter concert he still thought you were his daughter. I mean, your name was clearly on the program as the violinist. Do you think it was a stretch?"

She watched the ambulance pull out of the school parking lot, turning on its lights as it went. "Some types of people see only what they want to see, regardless of the evidence in front of them. We can safely assume that Mr. Grieves is one of those people."

Bronnie took two lollipops from her jacket pocket and gave me a choice and then put the other back. Wrapping her hands behind her head, she leaned back on the vinyl seat and closed her eyes.

"I like you, Bronnie, but you are completely insane."

Bronnie nudged me with her elbow. "Thank you for the compliment."

Epilogue:

May 1, 2018

A letter arrived in the mail today, addressed to my business. At first I thought it was a wedding invitation, the paper was so thick and writing elegant. As I opened it, a folded news clipping fell onto the floor. When I began to read, my legs went numb. So I finished the letter while sitting on my kitchen floor.

Elizabeth Correa
Naiad Swim and Scuba Academy
3426 Aegis Avenue
Redcliffe 4020
Queensland, Australia

April 22, 2018

Dear Elizabeth and Bethany,

I do hope this letter finds you both safe and well. It was originally my intention not to directly contact you regarding what has happened in your former hometown this year, however since you were not present at the trial, I assumed you had not heard the good news.

Emmanuel Grieves was arrested in early February on the charge of First Degree Kidnapping With A Firearm (along with various accompanying felonies and misdemeanors). As you might be aware, in our state a first class felony carries a minimum sentence of ten years in prison. Based on

Emmanuel's past record of flight from prosecution and his preoccupation with you both, the judge would not grant the possibility of parole.

Bethany should be well out of college before he even has a chance of seeing the other side of the prison wall.

Also, the prosecutor is intending to press the original assault, battery and child abuse charges from so many years ago. Your presence at the trial obviously would be most advantageous.

If you are hesitant to return, it may be worth noting that, at the latest trial, Emmanuel was making use of the public defender rather than a private attorney. The likelihood of him mounting any kind of formidable defense is slim. As would be his ability to pay a third party for any kind of retribution against.

Jennifer Faraday can fill you in with any further details you may require. She was integral in keeping Emmanuel off your trail these long years.

I am also, as far as I know, the only person who knows your current location and will be destroying any evidence to that effect the moment I mail this letter.

I wish you both a peaceful and very happy future.

Most sincerely,

BB

Enclosure